TO THE BUGS ISSUE

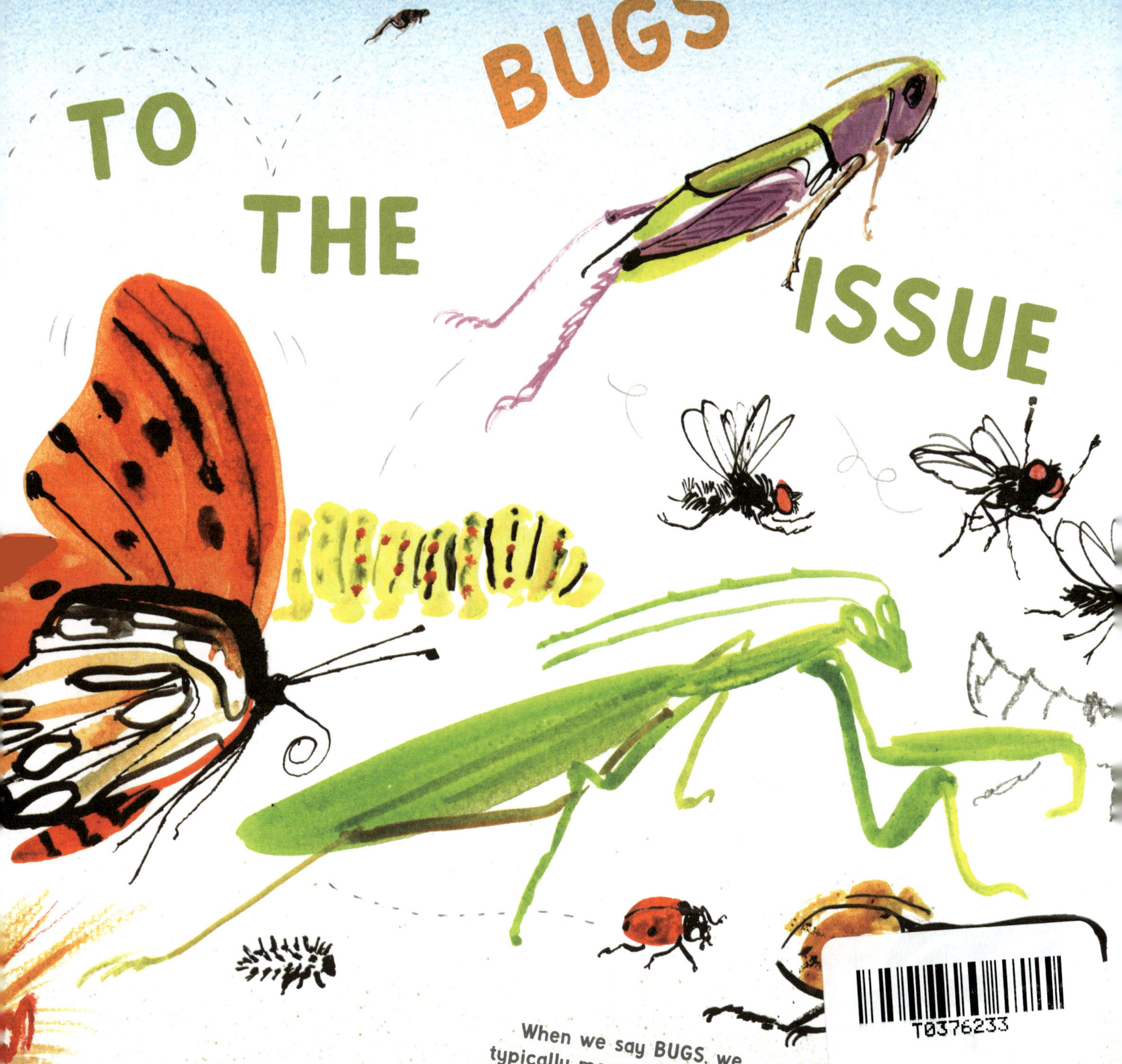

In this issue devoted to the tiniest heroes that keep our planet humming, we'll take a magnifying glass and extend a curious gaze to the wonderful world of bugs.

When we say BUGS, we typically mean ANY crawling, creeping, zipping, buzzing tiny thing. The subject can delight or disgust... or terrify!

Learn how to talk about bugs, write about bugs, even dress like one. You could even get a job studying bugs as a future entomologist.

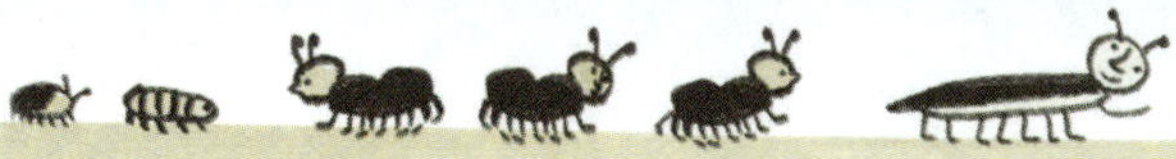

FROM US TO YOU...

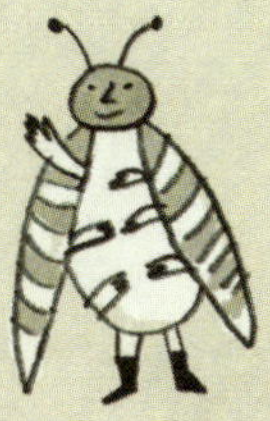

WE ASKED OUR CONTRIBUTORS:
NAME A BUG THAT IS ON YOUR BUCKET LIST OR ONE THAT WOULD GIVE YOU A THRILL TO SEE IN REAL LIFE SOMEDAY.

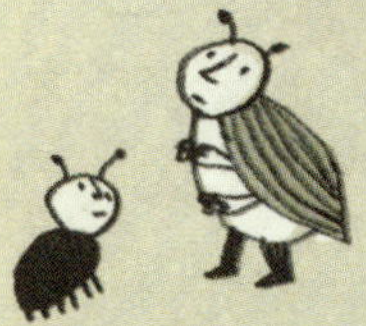

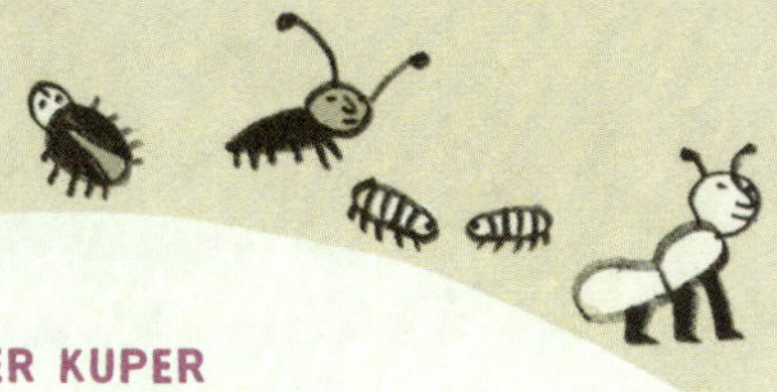

PETER KUPER
Goliath beetle

JESSIXA BAGLEY
Giant moth

SOPHIA MARTINECK
The European stag beetle. I love their marvelous pair of antlers.

LAUREN TAMAKI
I would love to see an orchid mantis! So pink! So pretty!

YUK FUN
Fireflies! We don't get them in the UK.

DARIN SHULER
The rosy maple moth

TOM BINGHAM
The orchid mantis. It looks like a flower!

WENG PIXIN
The rainbow battleship caterpillar. It has an AMAZING name, and it looks super cool to boot (from the pictures I see online).

ZACHARIAH OHORA
A giant walking stick

JACOPO RICCARDI
The bagworm moth caterpillar because it builds miniature log cabins out of twigs on its back.

YULIA DROBOVA
Chrysina limbata (metallic silver beetle)

KATHARINA KULENKAMPFF
Goliath beetle

CHARLOTTE AGER
Blue morpho butterfly

AARON BAGLEY
I'd love to spot a stick bug in the wild.

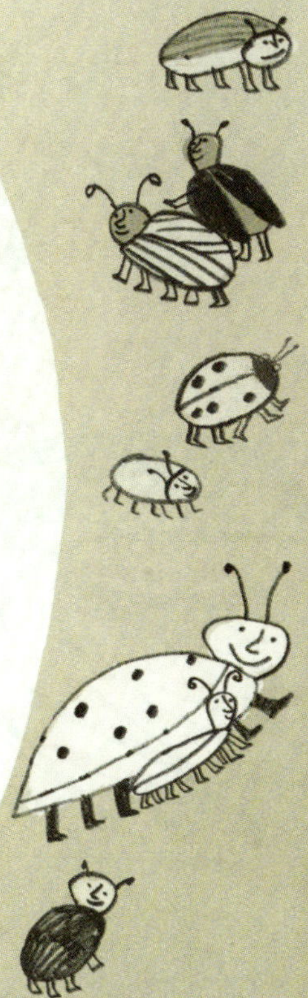

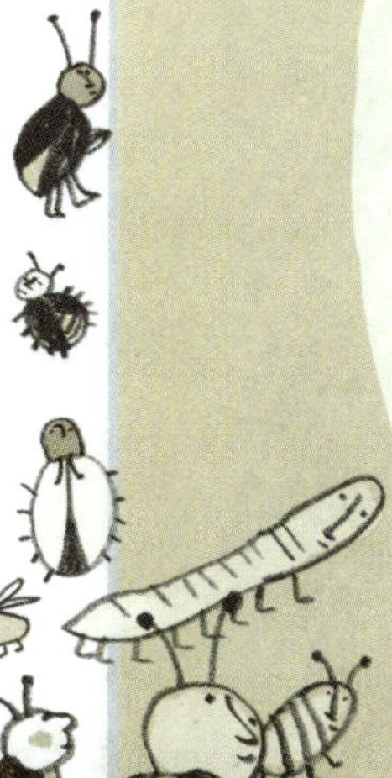

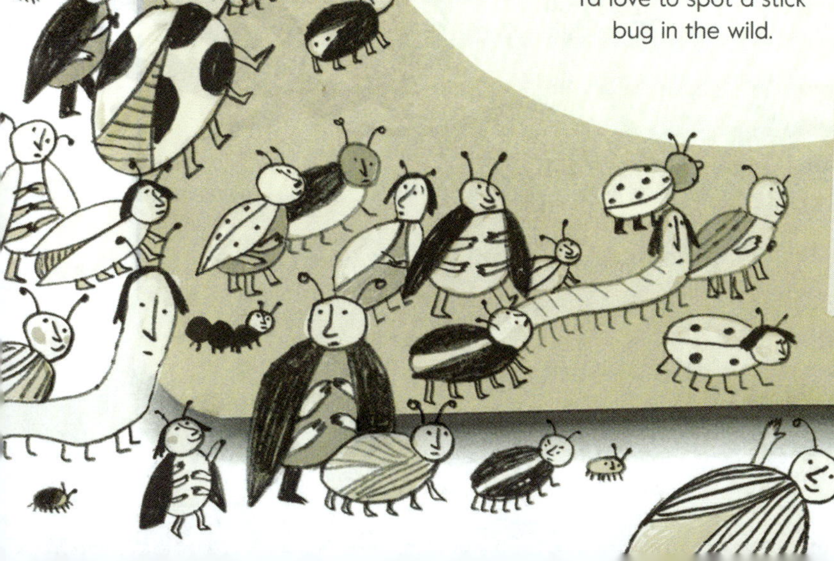

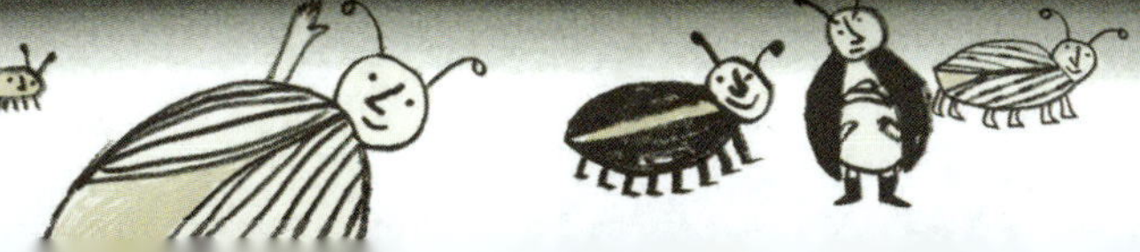

from our youth advisors:

LANIYAH
Definitely an orchid mantis, I like the pink color!

EVELYN
A praying mantis

JOSH
I would love to see a giant swallowtail butterfly.

from our youth advisors:

LANIYAH
Roaches and centipedes... BIG no...

JOSH
I never want to be around wasps again.

EVELYN
Flies

AND ALSO:

TELL US WHICH BUG YOU WOULD HAPPILY NEVER SEE AGAIN, IF YOU COULD MAGICALLY AVOID IT FOR THE REST OF YOUR LIFE?

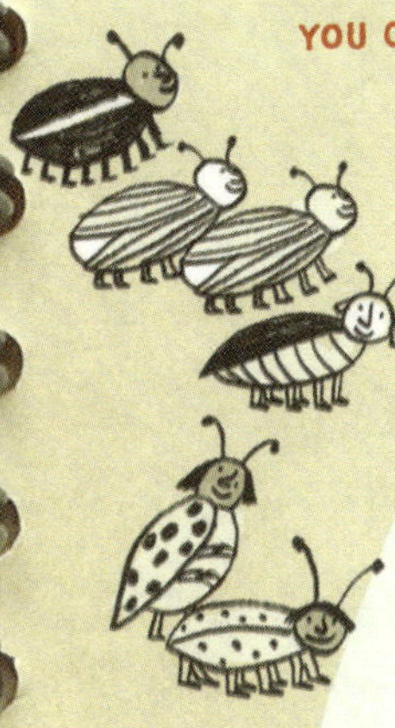

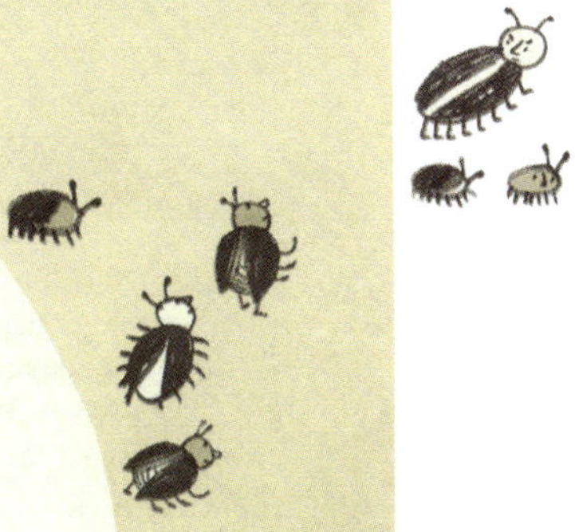

LAUREN TAMAKI
I've had many cockroach roommates in my day and it's eviction time!

SOPHIA MARTINECK
Cockroaches send me over the edge.

DARIN SHULER
The Amazonian giant centipede. Gross!

PETER KUPER
Biting midge

CHARLOTTE AGER
Silverfish

JACOPO RICCARDI
The human botfly. Parasites are one of the things that terrify me the most.

TOM BINGHAM
Hornets. Scary!

ZACHARIAH OHORA
Mosquitoes

JESSIXA BAGLEY
Spiders!

YULIA DROBOVA
Amazonian giant centipede

WENG PIXIN
I would love to magically never encounter any type of mosquitoes or sandflies!

KATHARINA KULENKAMPFF
Wolf spiders

YUK FUN
Fungus gnats

AARON BAGLEY
A scorpion, while highly intriguing, is not a bug I want to share space with.

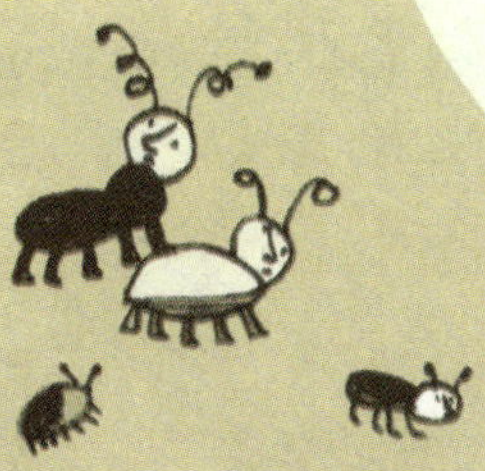

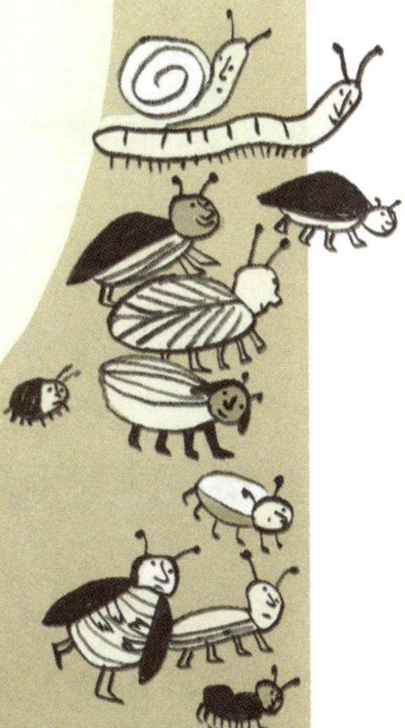

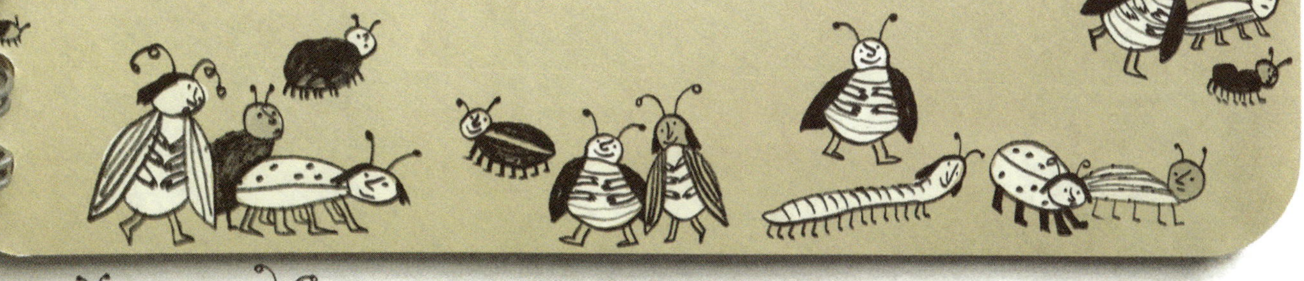

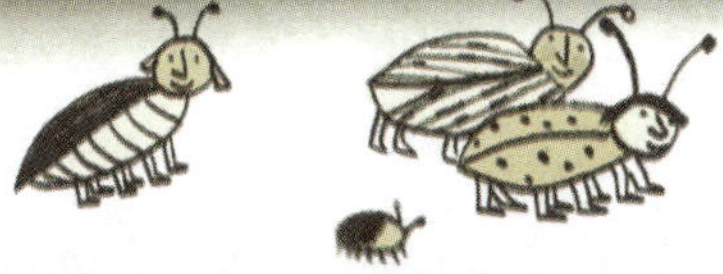

ART BY CHARLOTTE AGER

inside iLLUSTORiA

MEET special guests

cover artist
JESÚS CISNEROS

guest writers
JESSIXA & AARON BAGLEY

welcome page
LAUREN TAMAKI

typographic artist
YULIA DROBOVA

chapter artist
KATHARINA KULENKAMPFF

CHAPTER 1
COMPLETE NONSENSE

Chapter Comics 6
art by Katharina Kulenkampff

What Makes a Bug a Bug? 8
by Michael Buchino

Word Sleuth 10
by Jacopo Riccardi

Creepy-Crawly Quagmire 12
art by Sophia Martineck

Say What!? 14
art by Weng Pixin

Story Starters 16
art by Sophia Martineck

GRAB A FRIEND AND TRY THESE!

CHAPTER 2
~~NONE~~ SOME OF YOUR BUSINESS

Chapter Comics 18
art by Katharina Kulenkampff

Louse of Style 20
by Lauren Tamaki

Dora the Beekeeper 24
by YUK FUN

Dungeons & Dragonflies 26
words by Aaron Bagley
art by Andy Chou Musser

Process Interview 28
with Peter Kuper

Small Talk: Factoids 34
curated by Lauren Tamaki

Interview with our Cover Artist 36
with Jesús Cisneros

Carl the Collector: Ant Farm .. 42
by Zachariah Ohora

CHAPTER 3

projects to make that will astound

Chapter Comics	46
art by Katharina Kulenkampff	
DogChef: Peanut Butter Snails	48
by Tom Bingham	
Draw This	50
photo by Jurgen Otto	
Make This	52
with Weng Pixin and Aaron Piland	
Drawn by You	54
art by students around the world	
Youth Writing	56
art by Darin Shuler	
words by Raku Shinagawa	
Youth Writing	58
art by Darin Shuler	
words by Ammaar Ibrahim	

THE BUGS ISSUE

CHAPTER 4

~~Don't~~ Try This At Home

Chapter Comics	62
art by Katharina Kulenkampff	
On Our Playlist	64
On Our Desk	65
with Weng Pixin	
Book Review Contest	66
by Sayuri Dinoop and Vera Traer	
On Our Bookshelf	68

EXTRAS

Deeper Dive

Deeper Dive	70
tips for curiosity-fueled tangents and further reading	

- Try this brilliant red paint made from the cochineal insect.
- Essential tools for future entomologists.
- Invent your own bugs with these stamps of insect body parts.

ILLUSTORIA IS THE OFFICIAL PUBLICATION OF THE INTERNATIONAL ALLIANCE OF YOUTH WRITING CENTERS

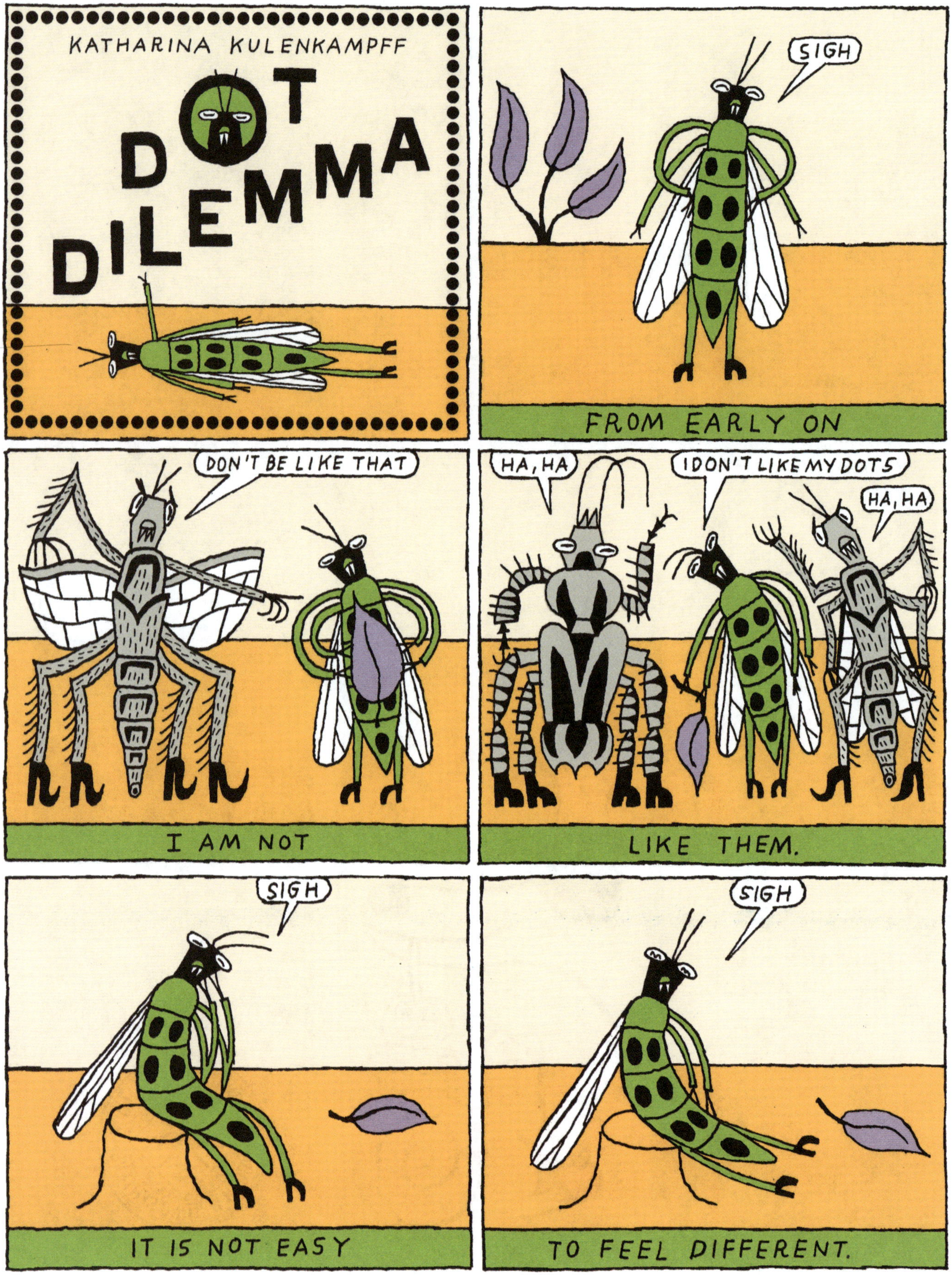
KATHARINA KULENKAMPFF
DOT DILEMMA
SIGH
FROM EARLY ON
DON'T BE LIKE THAT
I AM NOT
HA, HA
I DON'T LIKE MY DOTS
HA, HA
LIKE THEM.
SIGH
IT IS NOT EASY
SIGH
TO FEEL DIFFERENT.

CONTINUED ON PAGE 18

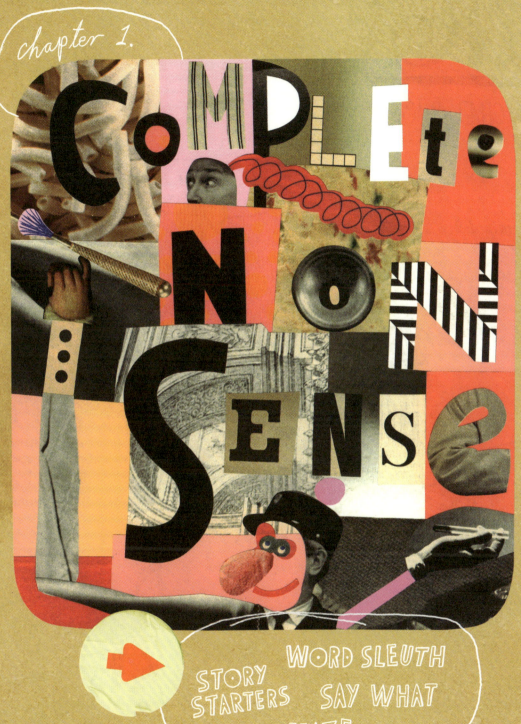

chapter 1.

COMPLETE NONSENSE

OUR CHAPTER PAGES FEATURE TYPOGRAPHIC ART BY YULIA DROBOVA

STORY STARTERS
WORD SLEUTH
SAY WHAT
MAZE

What makes a bug a BUG?

by MICHÆL BUCHINO

Bug is an inclusive, colloquial term for all manner of minibeasts and creepy crawlies, including insects, arachnids, crustaceans, myriapods, trilobites, worms, and microfauna. *What's your favorite bug feature?*

SHOES
DO YOU HAVE ½ A PAIR IN MY SIZE?

A *centipede* (Latin for *100 feet*) has 15 to 191 pairs of legs, or 30 to 382 total legs.

A *gastropod* (Greek for *stomach foot*), like snails and slugs, stores its guts above its single foot.

Japanese giant spider crabs (タカアシガニ taka·ashi·gani) have the largest leg-span of any arthropod—*up to 4 meters!*

A *microbiome* is a community of microorganisms living in a habitat, like inside and on the surface of your body.

A microbiome can include bacteria, fungi, algae, viruses, plasmids, and more.

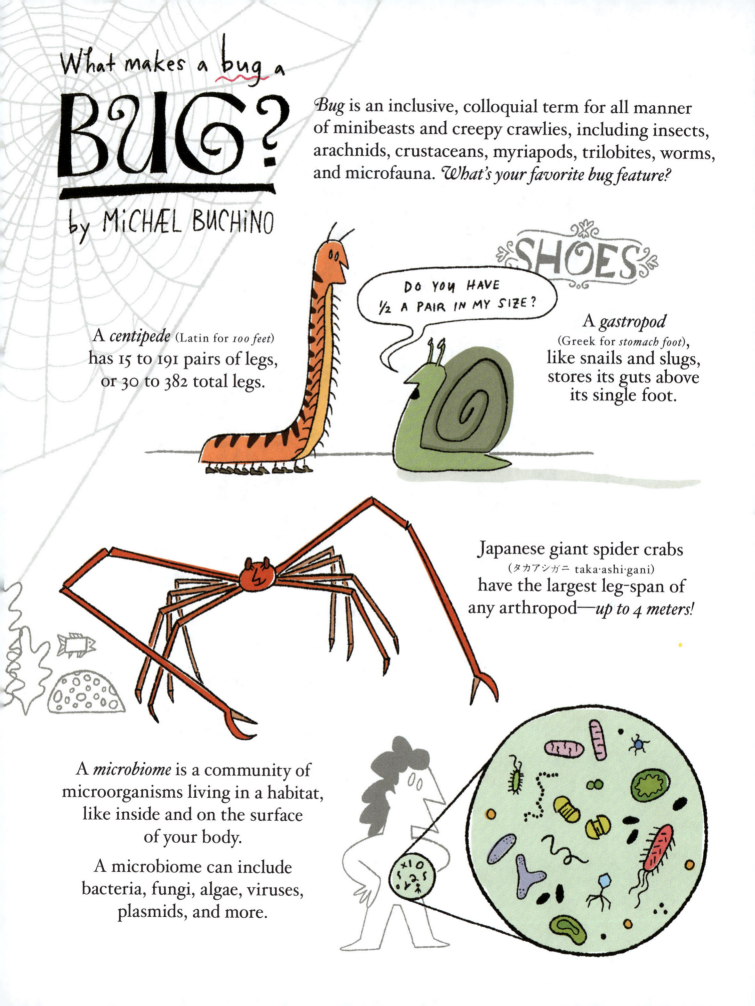

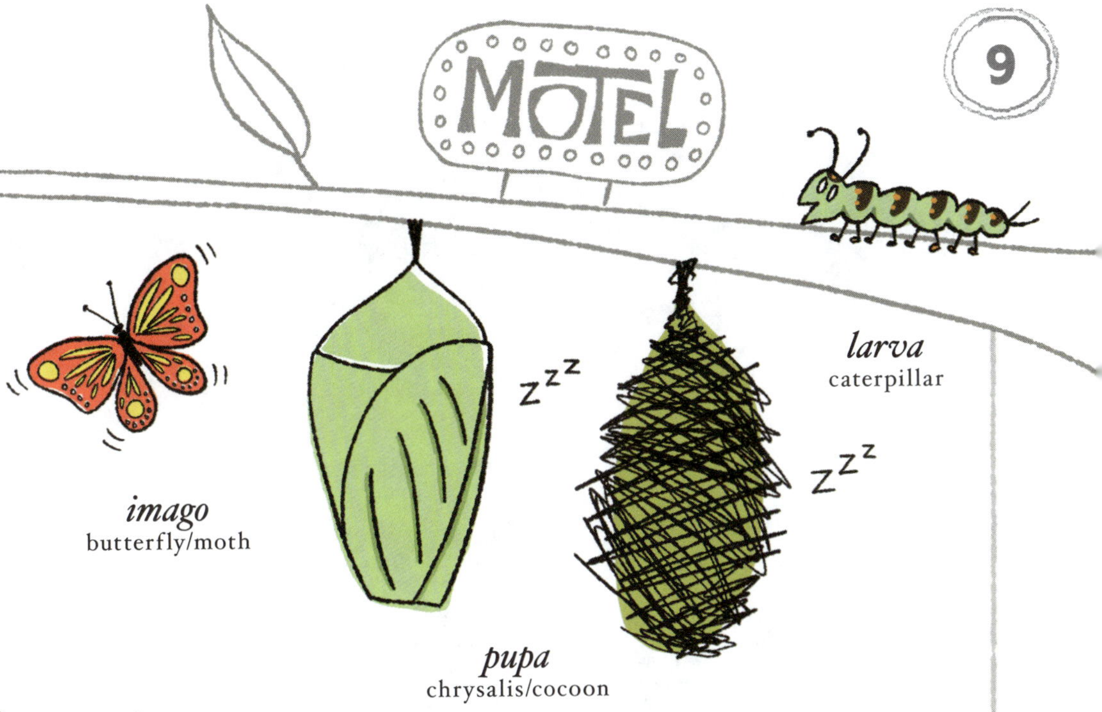
MOTEL
imago
butterfly/moth
pupa
chrysalis/cocoon
larva
caterpillar
z z z
z z z

During metamorphosis butterflies form a *chrysalis*, while moths make a *cocoon*.

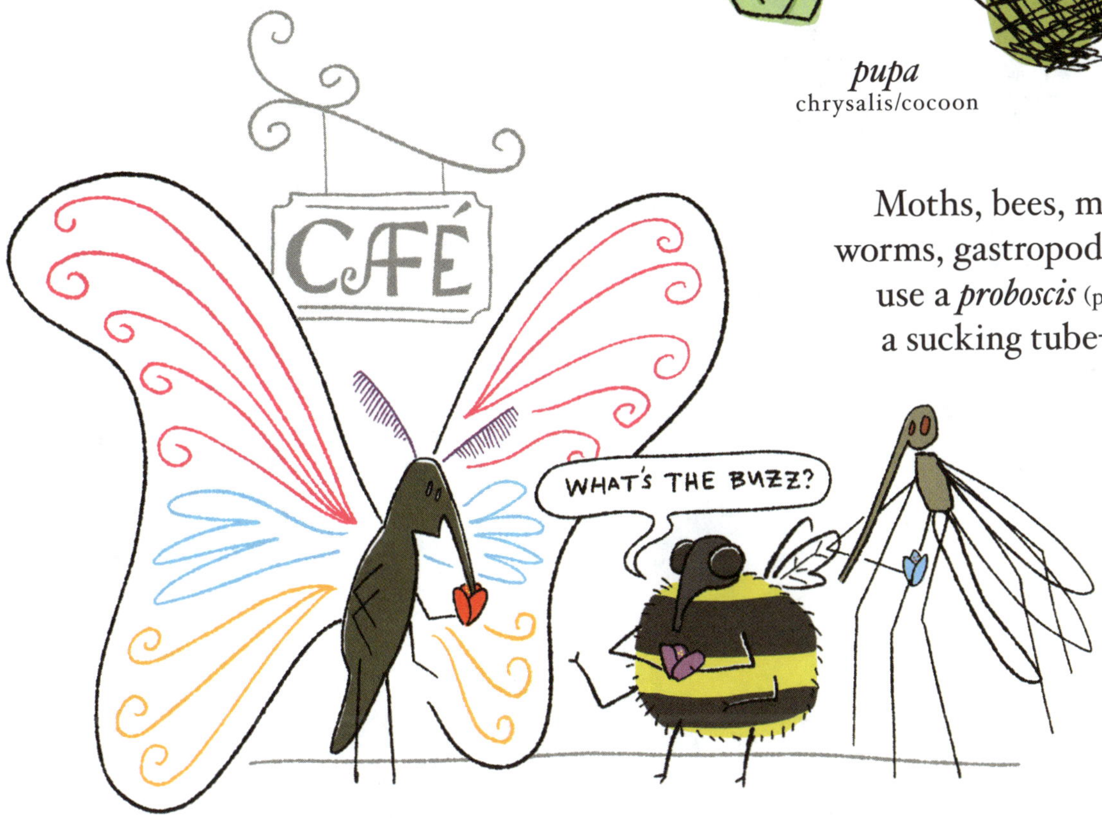
CAFÉ
WHAT'S THE BUZZ?

Moths, bees, mosquitoes, worms, gastropods, and others use a *proboscis* (pro·BOS·cis)—a sucking tube—to feed.

Elytra (EL·i·tra) are hardened forewings used as protective shells over beetles' hindwings, which are used for flying.

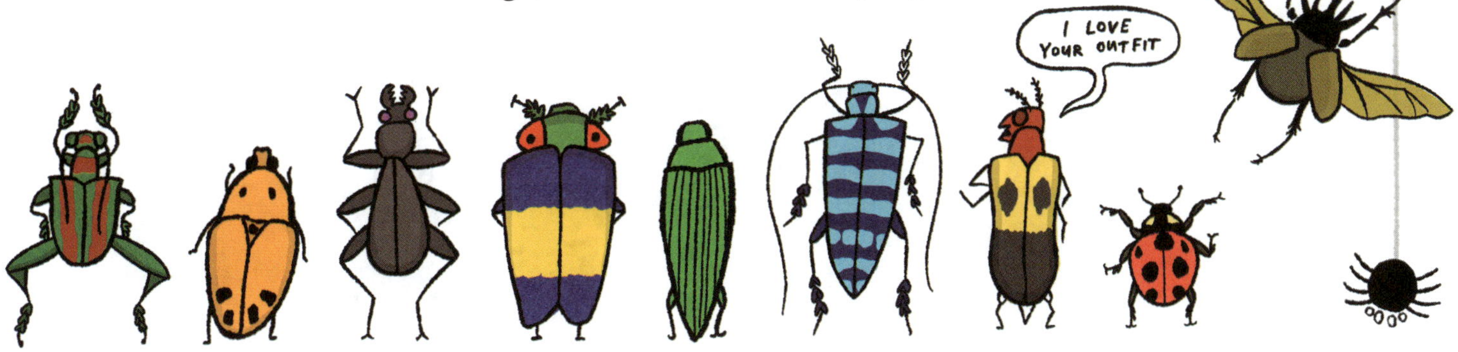
I LOVE YOUR OUTFIT

WORD SLEUTH →

collect the letters in RED to find a hidden message!

MUSIC IS IN THE EAR OF THE BEHOLDER

BY JACOPO RICCARDI

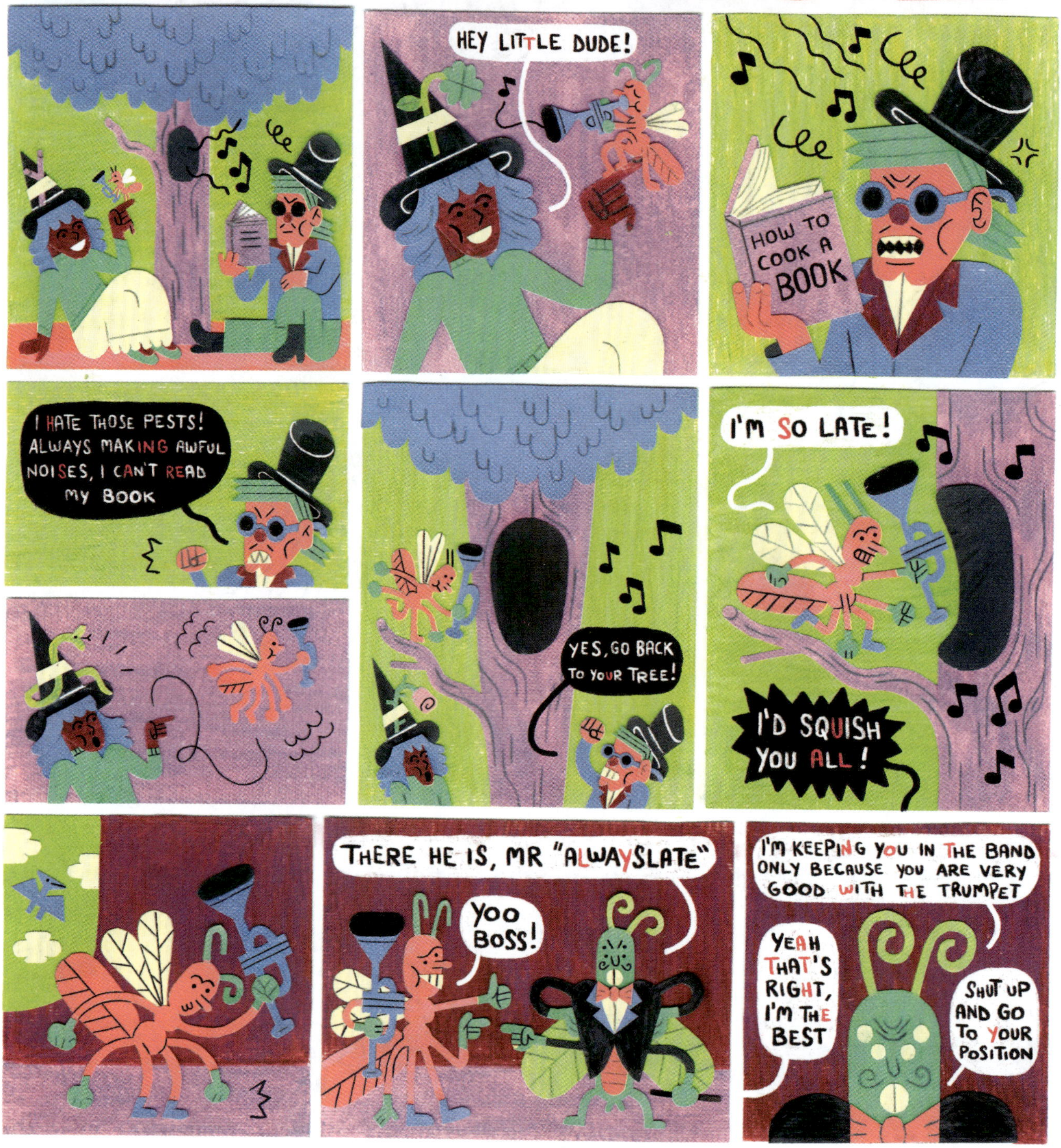
HEY LITTLE DUDE!
HOW TO COOK A BOOK
I HATE THOSE PESTS! ALWAYS MAKING AWFUL NOISES, I CAN'T READ MY BOOK
YES, GO BACK TO YOUR TREE!
I'M SO LATE!
I'D SQUISH YOU ALL!
THERE HE IS, MR "ALWAYSLATE"
YOO BOSS!
I'M KEEPING YOU IN THE BAND ONLY BECAUSE YOU ARE VERY GOOD WITH THE TRUMPET
YEAH THAT'S RIGHT, I'M THE BEST
SHUT UP AND GO TO YOUR POSITION

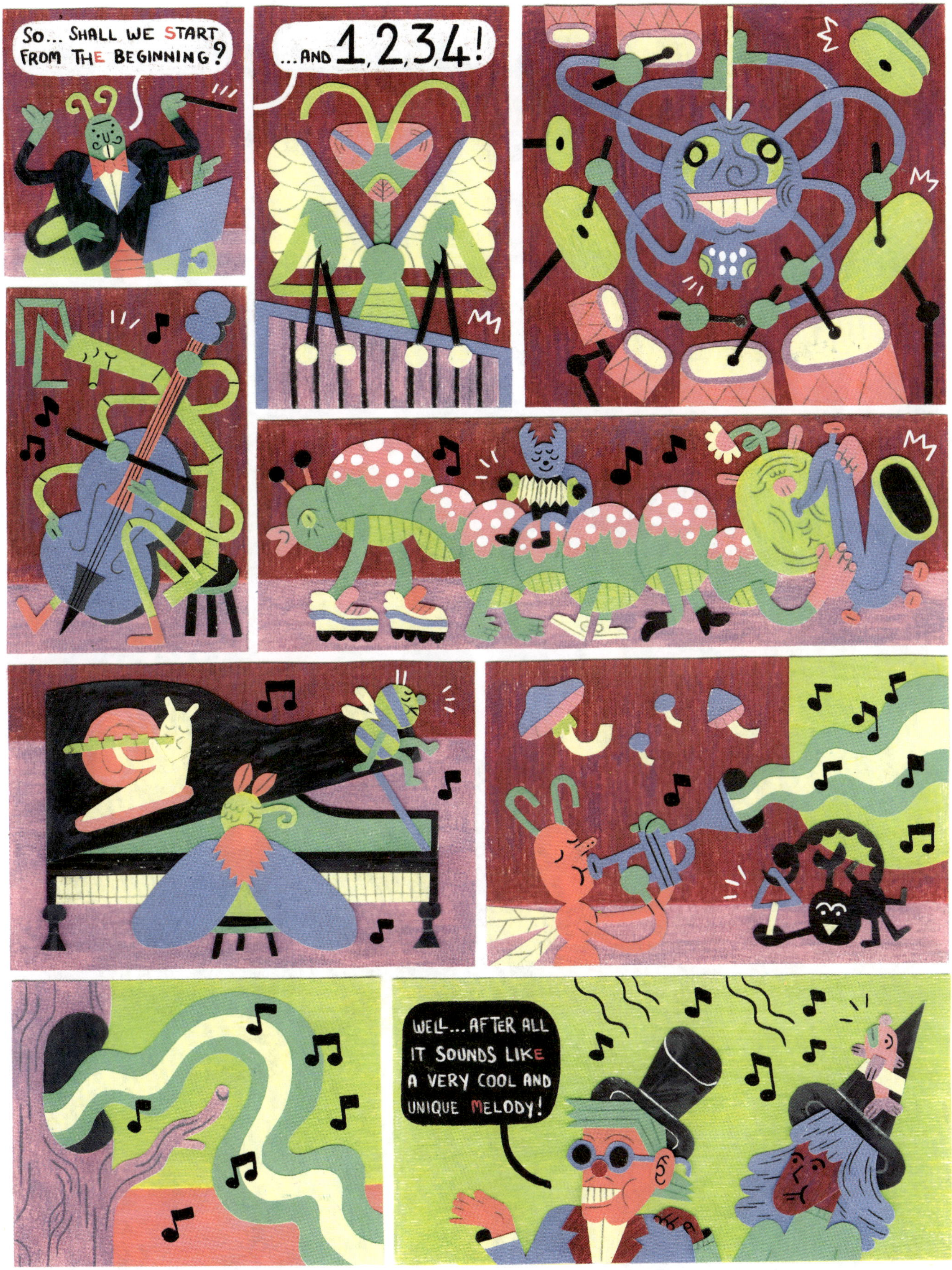
SO... SHALL WE START FROM THE BEGINNING?
...AND 1,2,3,4!
WELL... AFTER ALL IT SOUNDS LIKE A VERY COOL AND UNIQUE MELODY!

ANSWER: THINGS ARE USUALLY NOT WHAT THEY SEEM

CREEPY-CRAWLY QUAGMIRE

maze by
SOPHIA MARTINECK

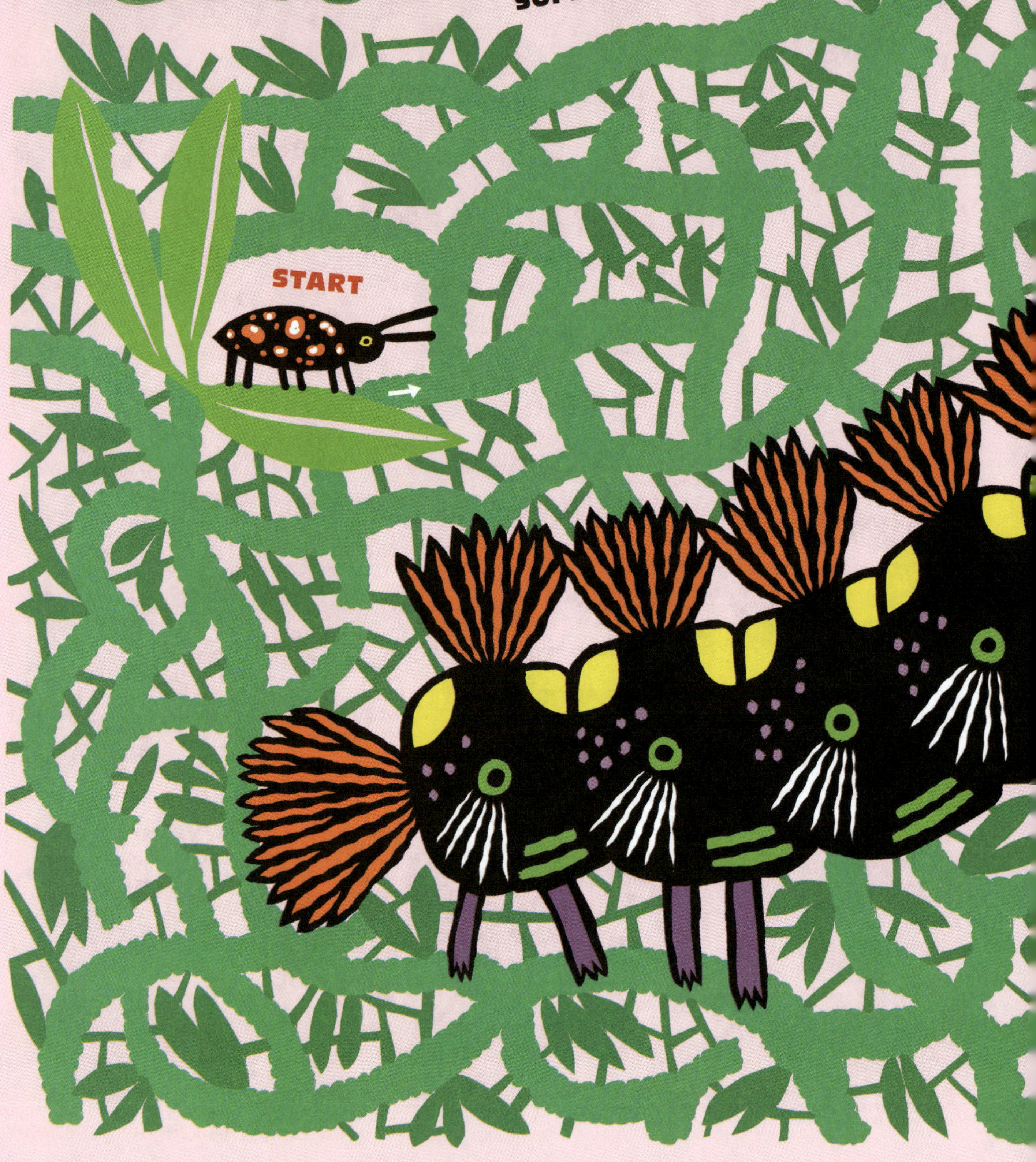
START

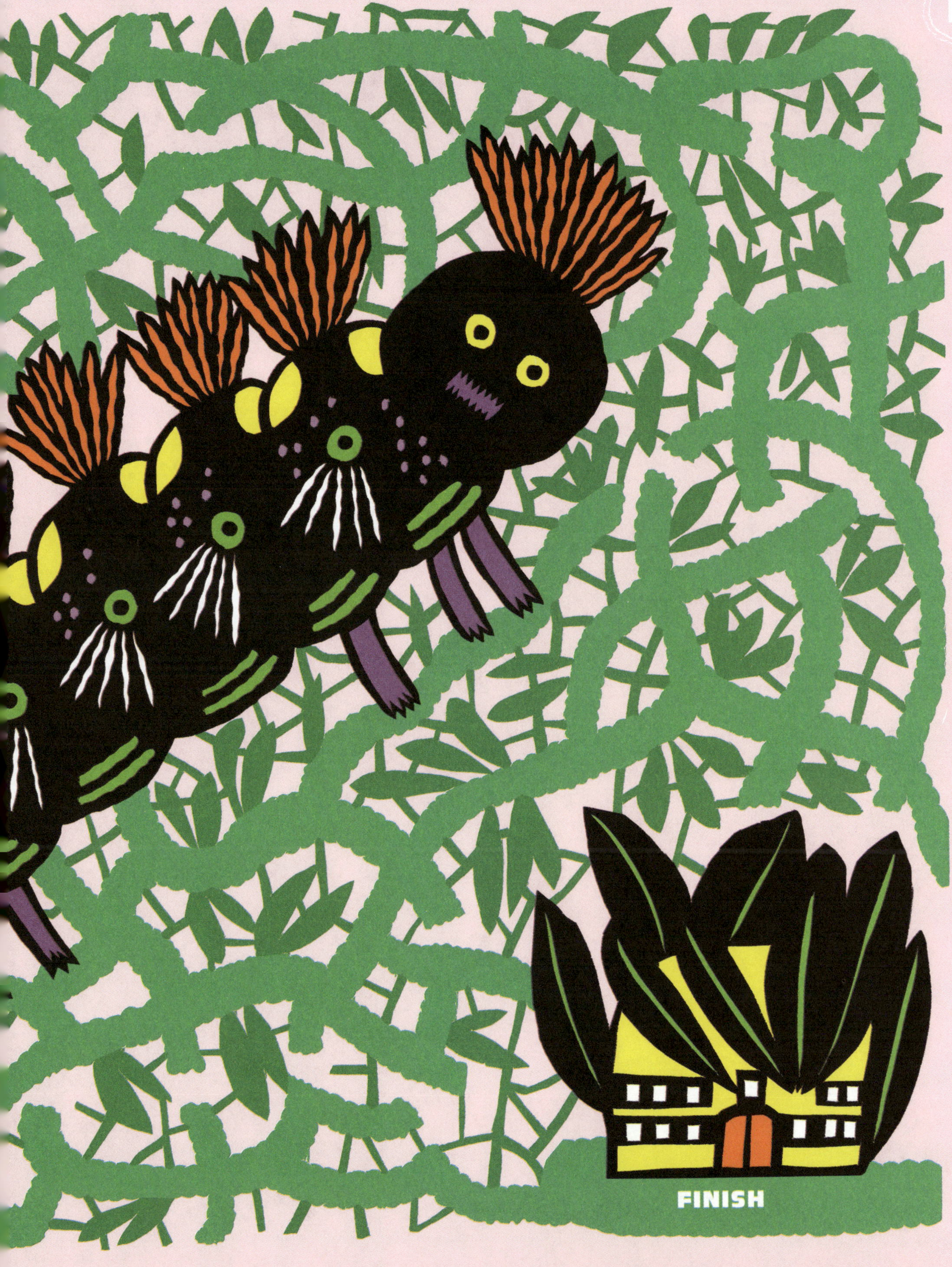
FINISH

SAY WHAT!?

MATCH THE SAYING TO THE BUG art by WENG PIXIN

Alone, and I'm likely gone. Together, we'll be strong.

I enjoy taking slow walks, gobbling tons of leaves, and accidentally stinging your pesky hands with my spikes.

I grapple with antlers, just like stags, but much smaller. Yet, I'm huge to some!

The humble acorn is my home. I lay my eggs in it through my trusty snout.

I love putting on my wizard hat with mystery orbs to scare away predators. Being weird keeps me alive.

You probably HATE me, but I LOVE you... and your blood.

We make meals from the fungus that grows on fresh-cut leaves that we harvest each day.

I chirp and screech in the day. Don't confuse me with Katydid, my night-shift colleague.

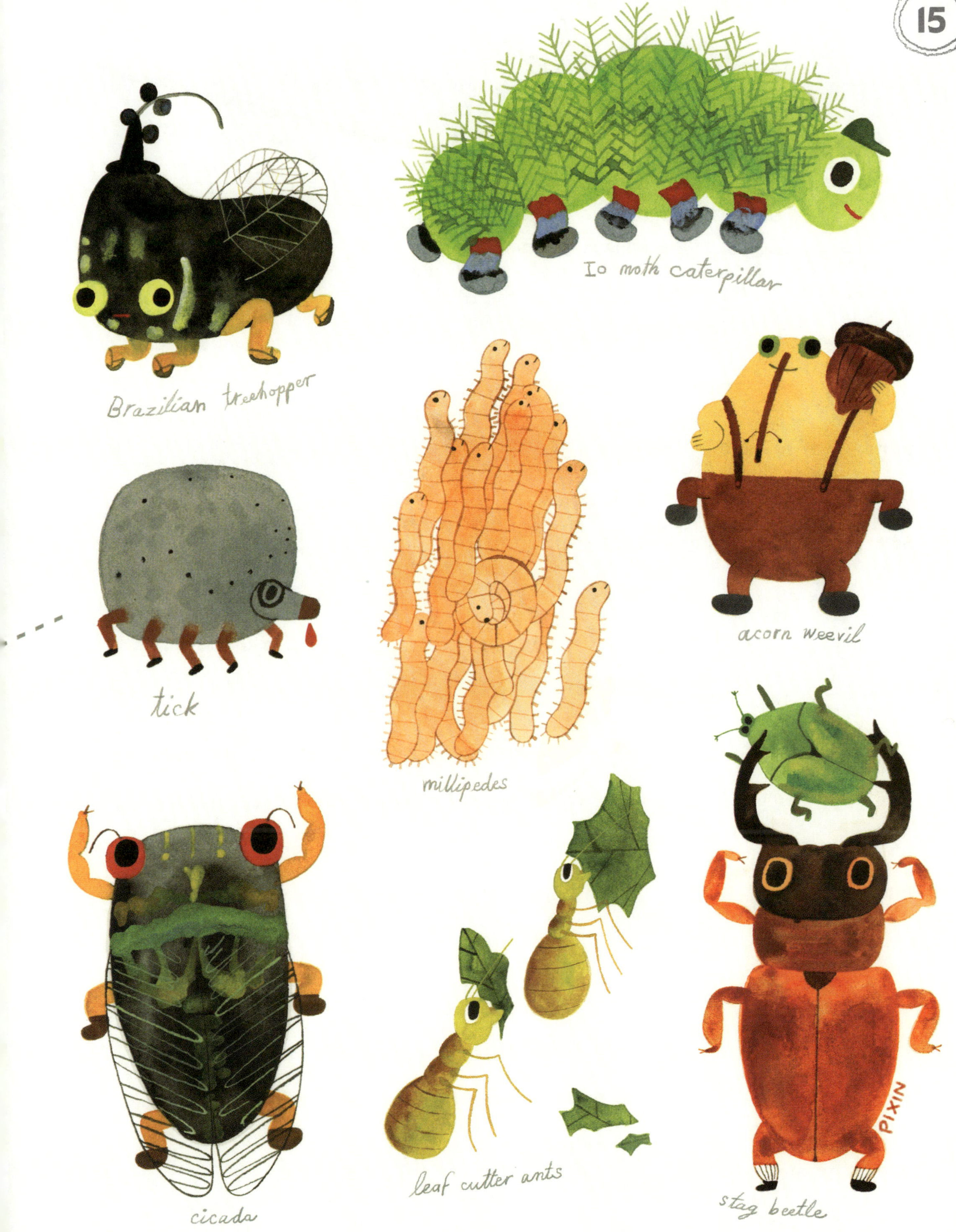
Io moth caterpillar
Brazilian treehopper
acorn weevil
tick
millipedes
cicada
leaf cutter ants
stag beetle
PIXIN

Story Starters > art by SOPHIA MARTINECK

**FILL IN THE BLANKS AND FINISH THIS TALE.
FIND A FRIEND TO HELP THINK UP STUFF.**

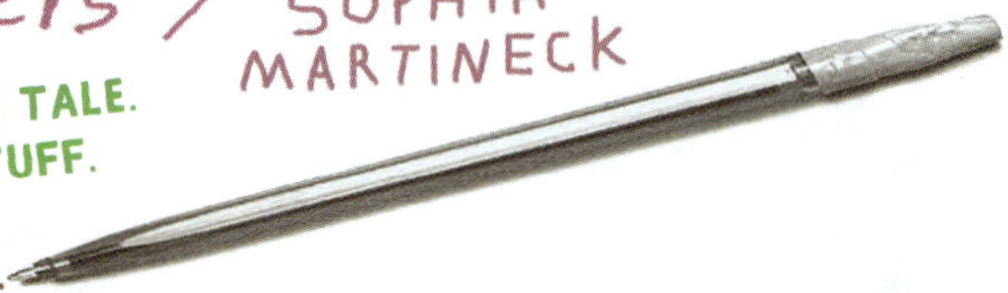

On ________________, the famous entomologist __________________, discovered a new
month, day, year *your math teacher's name*
species of moth. It's called the ________ + ______________ moth because of its habit
color *type of reptile*
of biting ___________________ on the ___________________ (even though the moth is
small animal, plural *body part*
vegetarian and harmless). Its scientific name is: __________________________________.
word in another language + your last name + IUS added at the end

In its larval stage, the caterpillar nibbles on ______________ and _________________.
plural fruit *plural vegetable*
In urban settings, it prefers to feast on _________________ and _________________.
type of candy *brand of soda*
As a survival strategy, it waves its ______________ antennae until every
adjective
____________________ vibrates with the same frequency. It can also enlarge its
item from the recycling bin
______________ until it becomes the size of __________________, so that even
part of a face *name of a planet*
a ____________________ is afraid of it.
type of predator

With a lifespan of _________ weeks, the first half is spent as a larva, with the pupa
number
stage lasting for _________ days. When the adult emerges from the cocoon, it flaps
number
its ________________ and communicates with other moths through ________________.
body part *type of dancing*
When the ________________ blooms on the second full moon, it's time for the moth to
specific flower
________________.
dangerous activity

It is not yet understood how the ___________________ finds its way home in the
name of your moth, from above
thick forests of ________________. Some theorize that a special sense organ in
name of country
the ____________________ helps them navigate, but skeptics think the insect reads
insect body part
___________________________ to collect information.
title of your favorite book

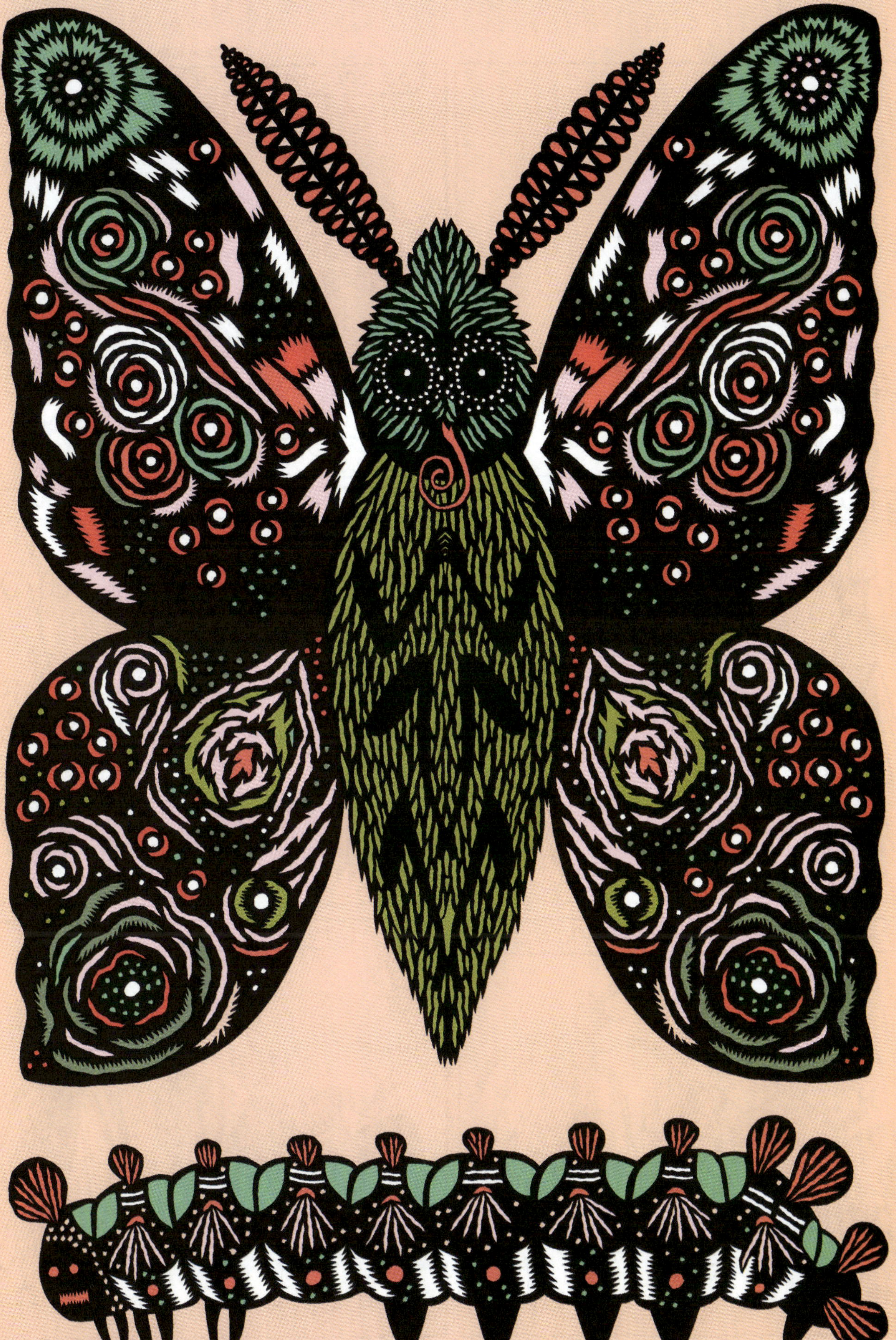

CONTINUED ON PAGE 46

KATHARINA KULENKAMPFF

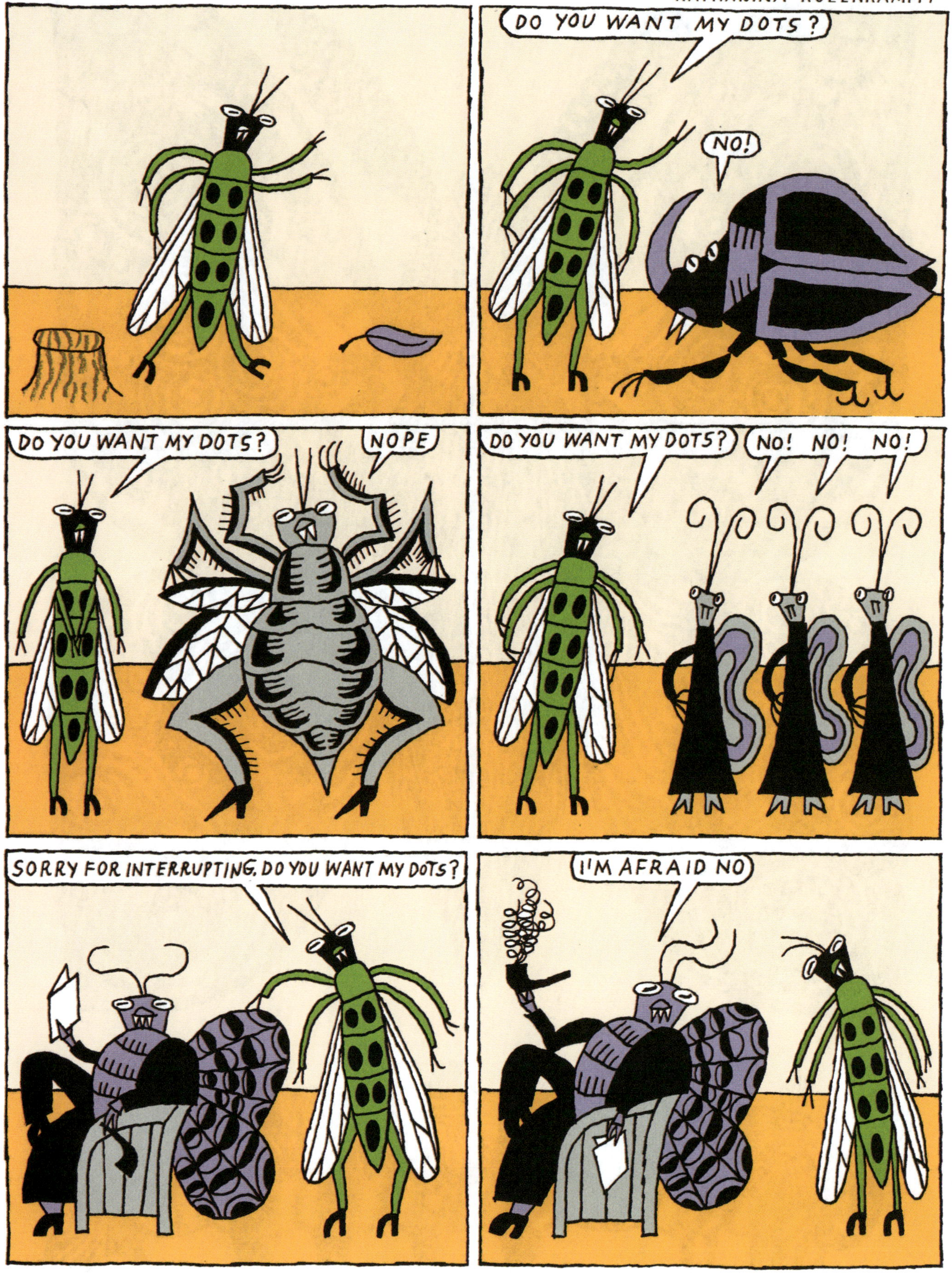
DO YOU WANT MY DOTS?
NO!
DO YOU WANT MY DOTS?
NOPE
DO YOU WANT MY DOTS?
NO! NO! NO!
SORRY FOR INTERRUPTING. DO YOU WANT MY DOTS?
I'M AFRAID NO

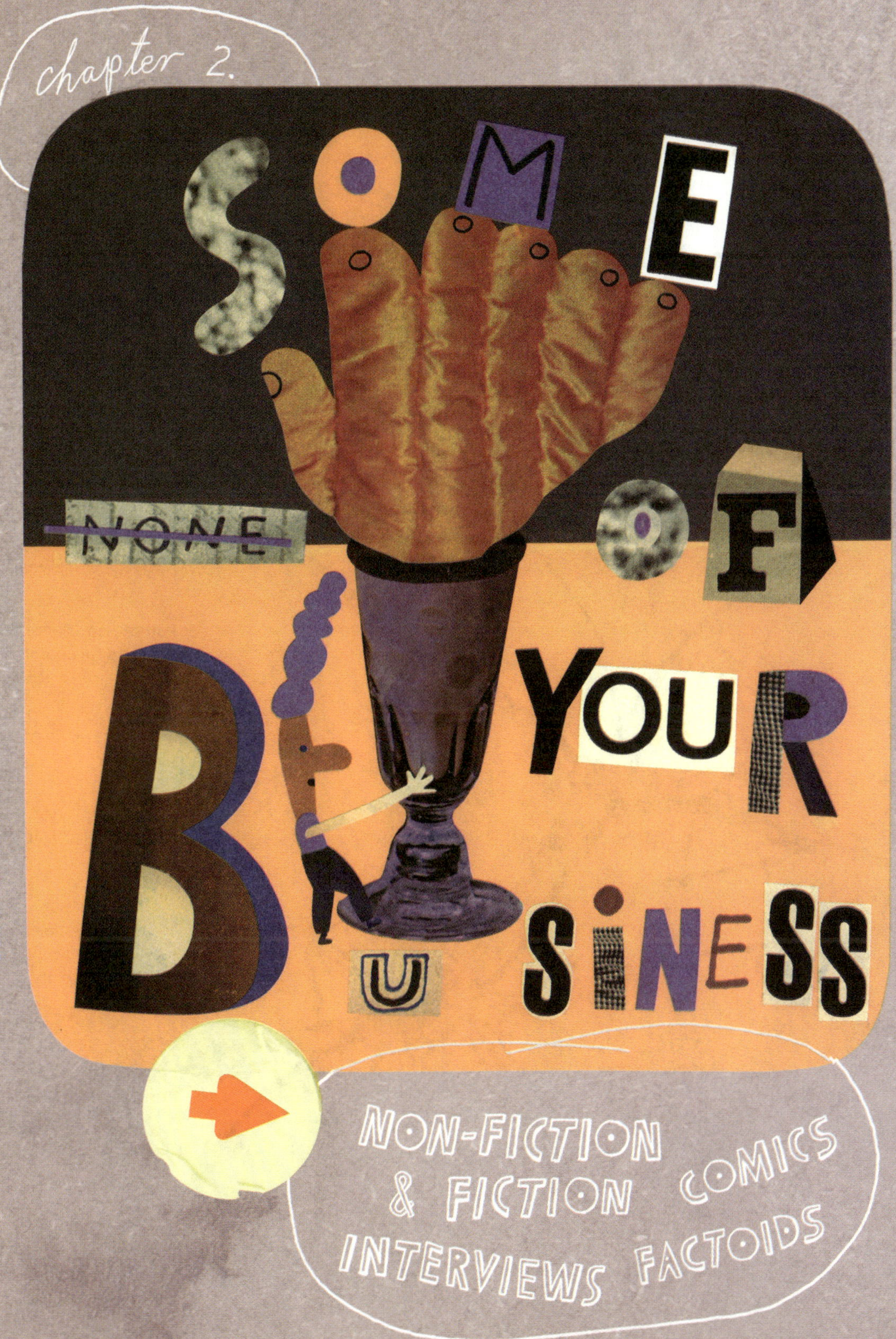
chapter 2.
SOME
~~NONE~~
OF
YOUR
BUSINESS
NON-FICTION
& FICTION
COMICS
INTERVIEWS
FACTOIDS

OUR CHAPTER PAGES FEATURE TYPOGRAPHIC ART BY YULIA DROBOVA

by LAUREN TAMAKI

LOUSE of STYLE

with BUG CUNNINGHAM!

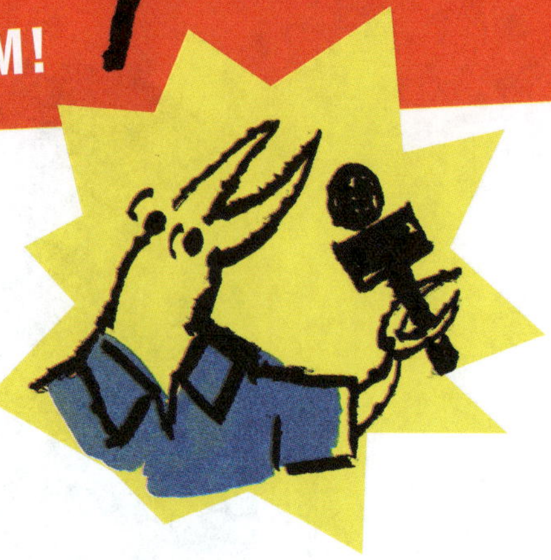

The best fashion show is definitely on the ground.

Excellent Exoskeletons! Captivating Chrysalises!

Let's delve into the twig-side trends, shall we?

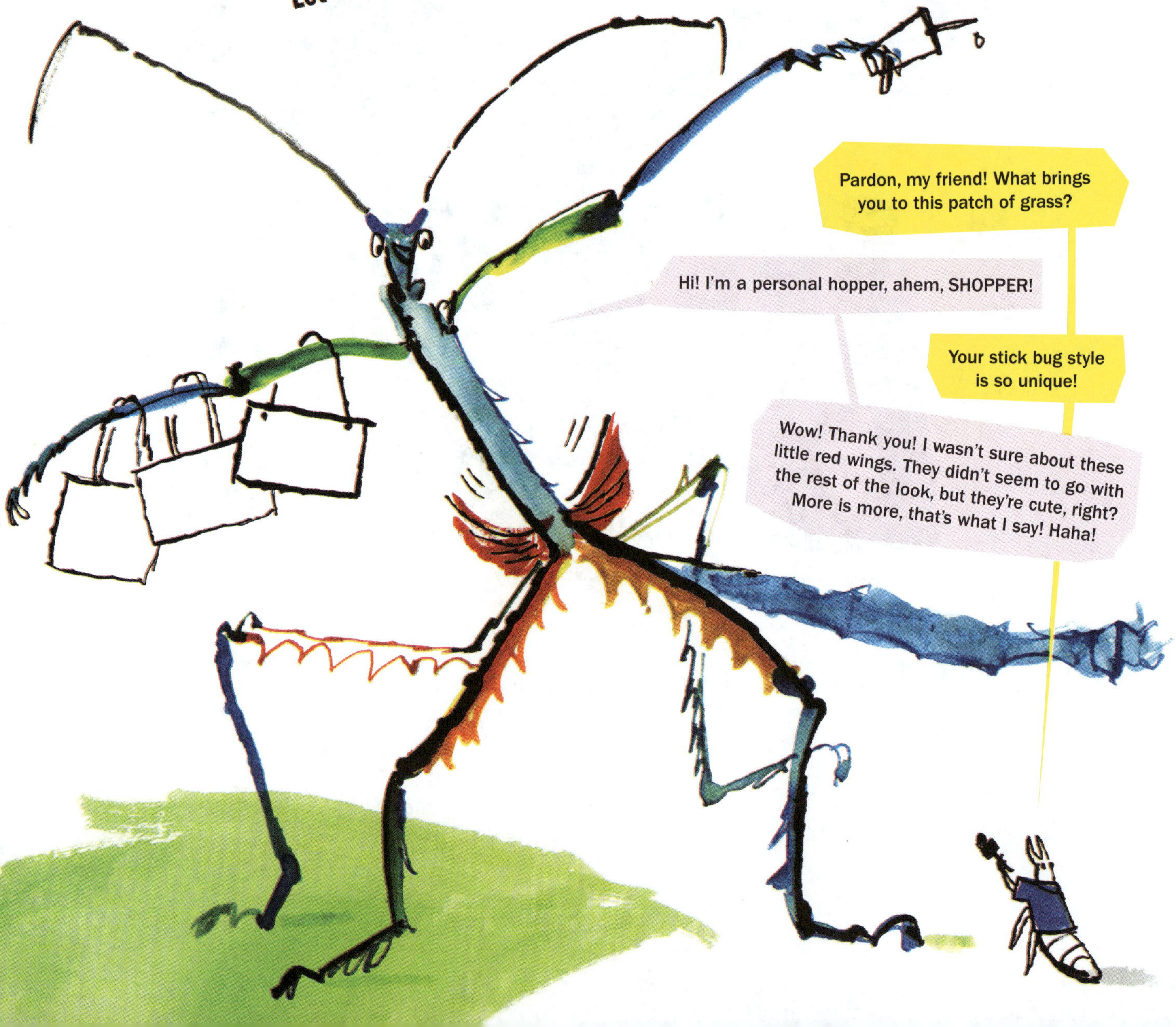
Pardon, my friend! What brings you to this patch of grass?
Hi! I'm a personal hopper, ahem, SHOPPER!
Your stick bug style is so unique!
Wow! Thank you! I wasn't sure about these little red wings. They didn't seem to go with the rest of the look, but they're cute, right? More is more, that's what I say! Haha!

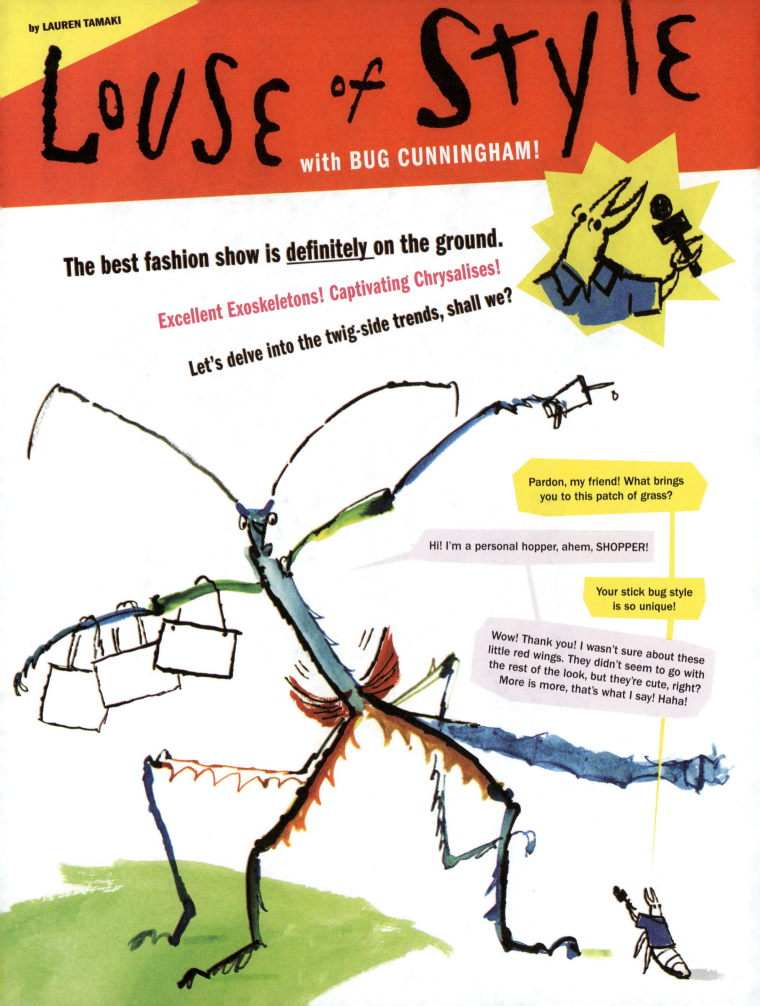

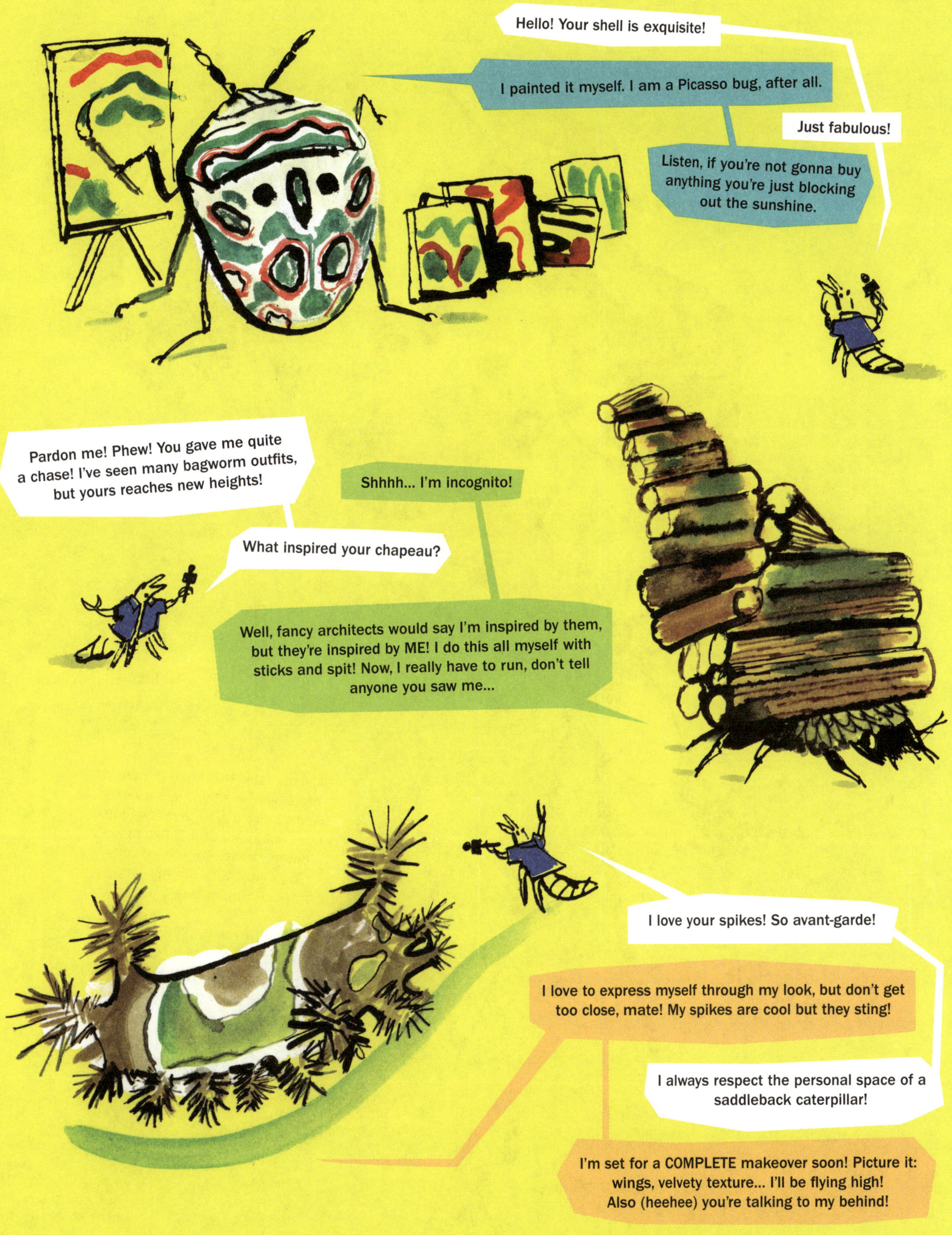
Hello! Your shell is exquisite!
I painted it myself. I am a Picasso bug, after all.
Just fabulous!
Listen, if you're not gonna buy anything you're just blocking out the sunshine.
Pardon me! Phew! You gave me quite a chase! I've seen many bagworm outfits, but yours reaches new heights!
Shhhh... I'm incognito!
What inspired your chapeau?
Well, fancy architects would say I'm inspired by them, but they're inspired by ME! I do this all myself with sticks and spit! Now, I really have to run, don't tell anyone you saw me...
I love your spikes! So avant-garde!
I love to express myself through my look, but don't get too close, mate! My spikes are cool but they sting!
I always respect the personal space of a saddleback caterpillar!
I'm set for a COMPLETE makeover soon! Picture it: wings, velvety texture... I'll be flying high! Also (heehee) you're talking to my behind!

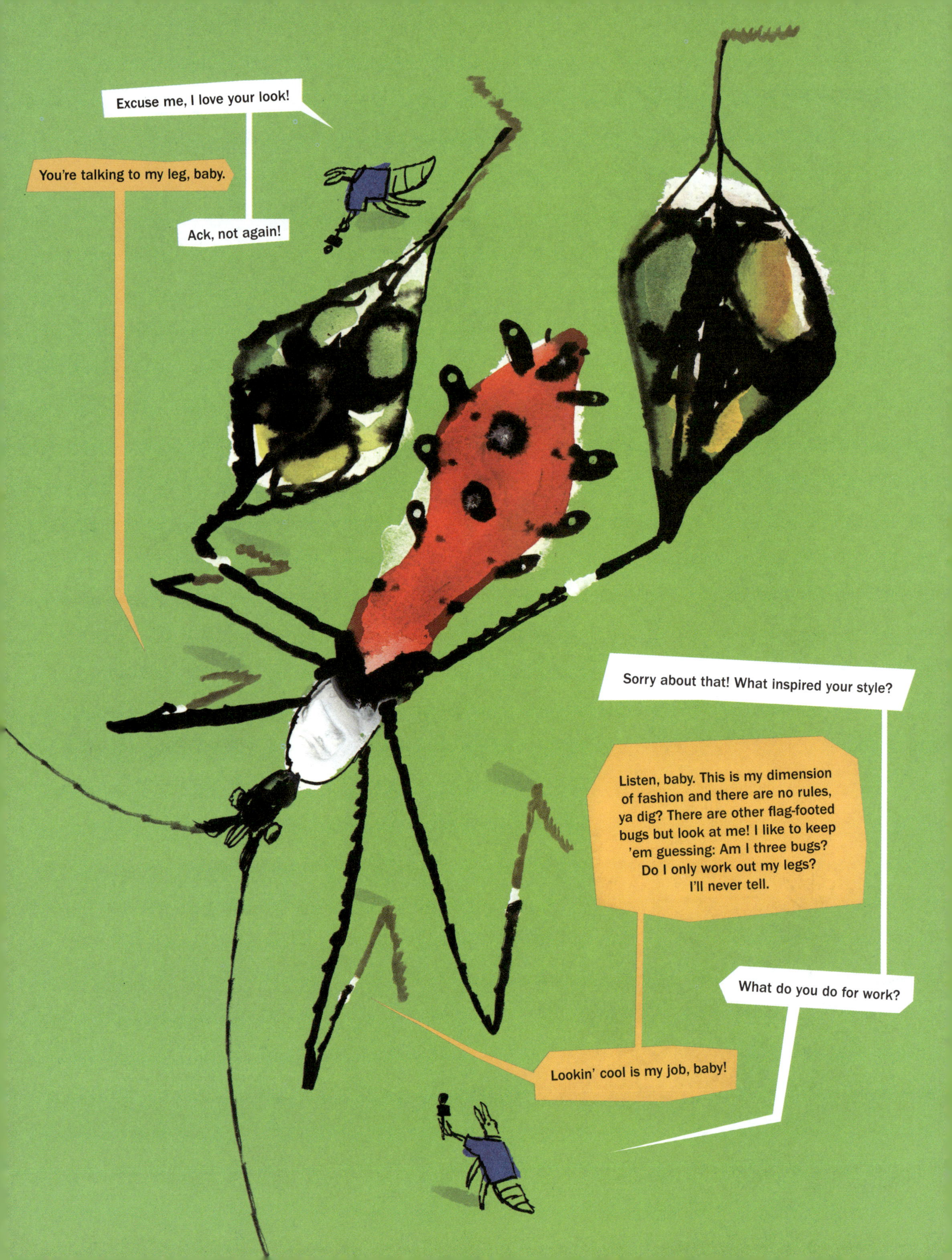
Excuse me, I love your look!
You're talking to my leg, baby.
Ack, not again!
Sorry about that! What inspired your style?
Listen, baby. This is my dimension of fashion and there are no rules, ya dig? There are other flag-footed bugs but look at me! I like to keep 'em guessing: Am I three bugs? Do I only work out my legs? I'll never tell.
What do you do for work?
Lookin' cool is my job, baby!

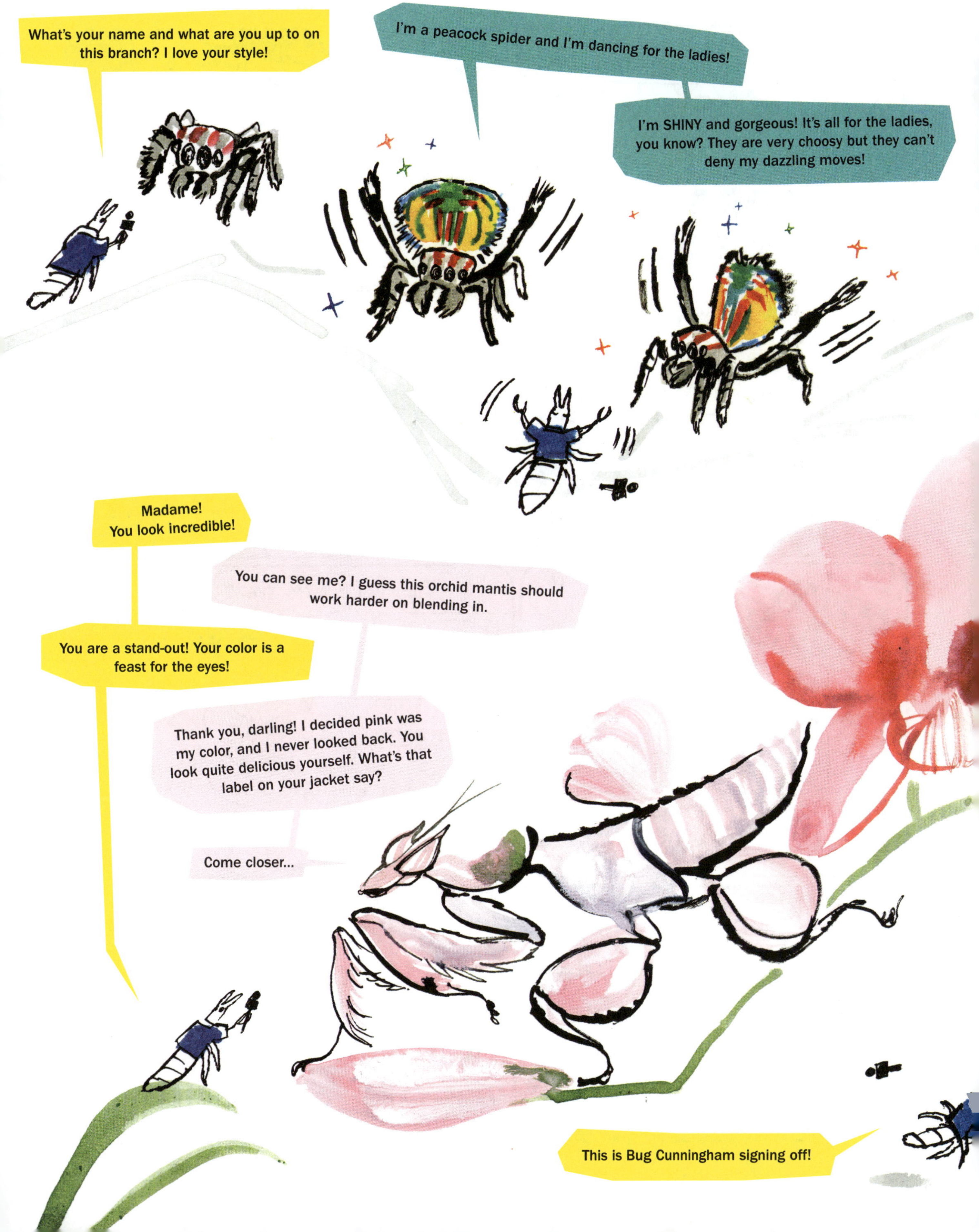
What's your name and what are you up to on this branch? I love your style!
I'm a peacock spider and I'm dancing for the ladies!
I'm SHINY and gorgeous! It's all for the ladies, you know? They are very choosy but they can't deny my dazzling moves!
Madame! You look incredible!
You can see me? I guess this orchid mantis should work harder on blending in.
You are a stand-out! Your color is a feast for the eyes!
Thank you, darling! I decided pink was my color, and I never looked back. You look quite delicious yourself. What's that label on your jacket say?
Come closer...
This is Bug Cunningham signing off!

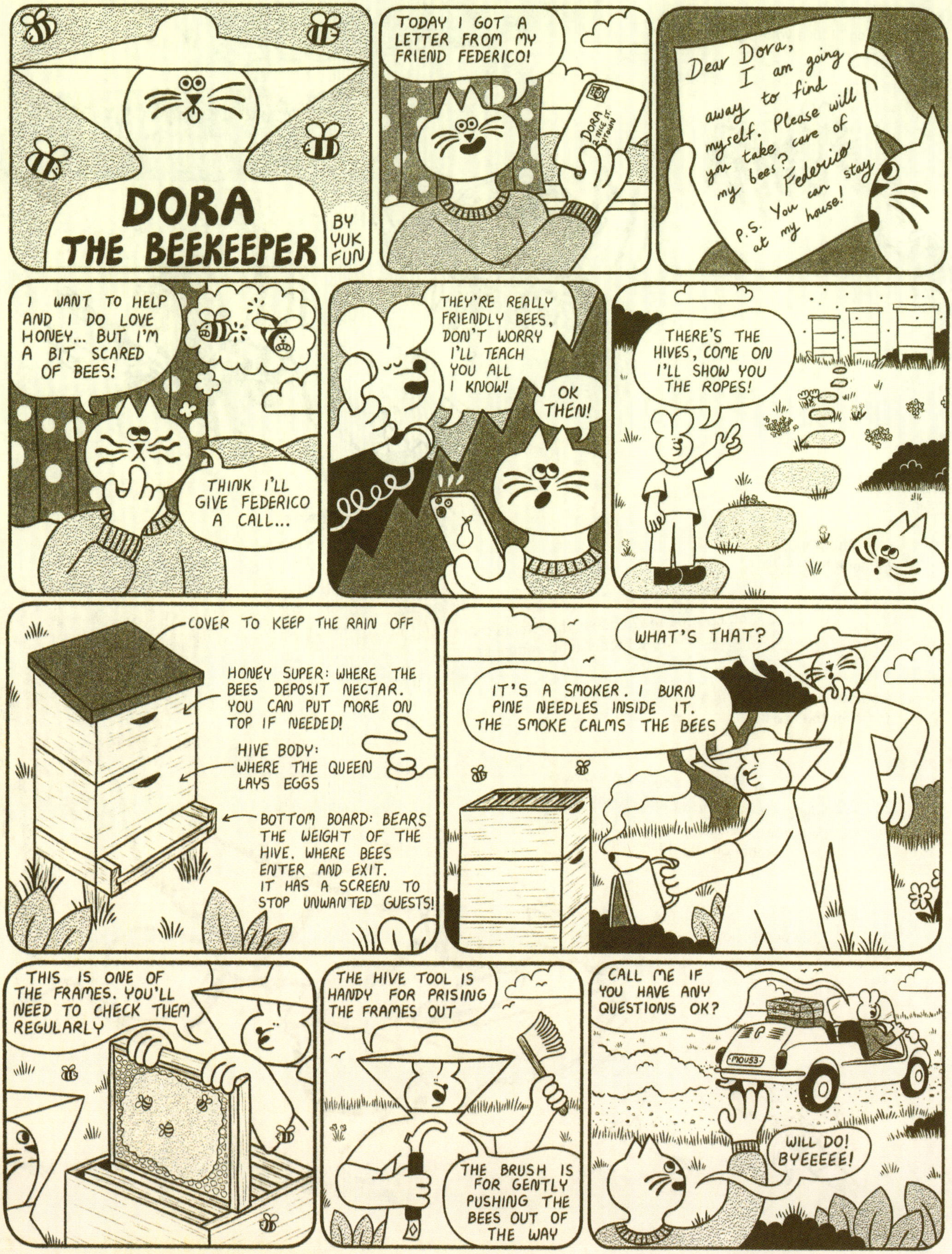
DORA THE BEEKEEPER
BY YUK FUN
TODAY I GOT A LETTER FROM MY FRIEND FEDERICO!
Dear Dora, I am going away to find myself. Please will you take care of my bees? Federico
P.S. You can stay at my house!
I WANT TO HELP AND I DO LOVE HONEY... BUT I'M A BIT SCARED OF BEES!
THINK I'LL GIVE FEDERICO A CALL...
THEY'RE REALLY FRIENDLY BEES, DON'T WORRY I'LL TEACH YOU ALL I KNOW!
OK THEN!
THERE'S THE HIVES, COME ON I'LL SHOW YOU THE ROPES!
COVER TO KEEP THE RAIN OFF
HONEY SUPER: WHERE THE BEES DEPOSIT NECTAR. YOU CAN PUT MORE ON TOP IF NEEDED!
HIVE BODY: WHERE THE QUEEN LAYS EGGS
BOTTOM BOARD: BEARS THE WEIGHT OF THE HIVE. WHERE BEES ENTER AND EXIT. IT HAS A SCREEN TO STOP UNWANTED GUESTS!
WHAT'S THAT?
IT'S A SMOKER. I BURN PINE NEEDLES INSIDE IT. THE SMOKE CALMS THE BEES
THIS IS ONE OF THE FRAMES. YOU'LL NEED TO CHECK THEM REGULARLY
THE HIVE TOOL IS HANDY FOR PRISING THE FRAMES OUT
THE BRUSH IS FOR GENTLY PUSHING THE BEES OUT OF THE WAY
CALL ME IF YOU HAVE ANY QUESTIONS OK?
WILL DO! BYEEEEE!

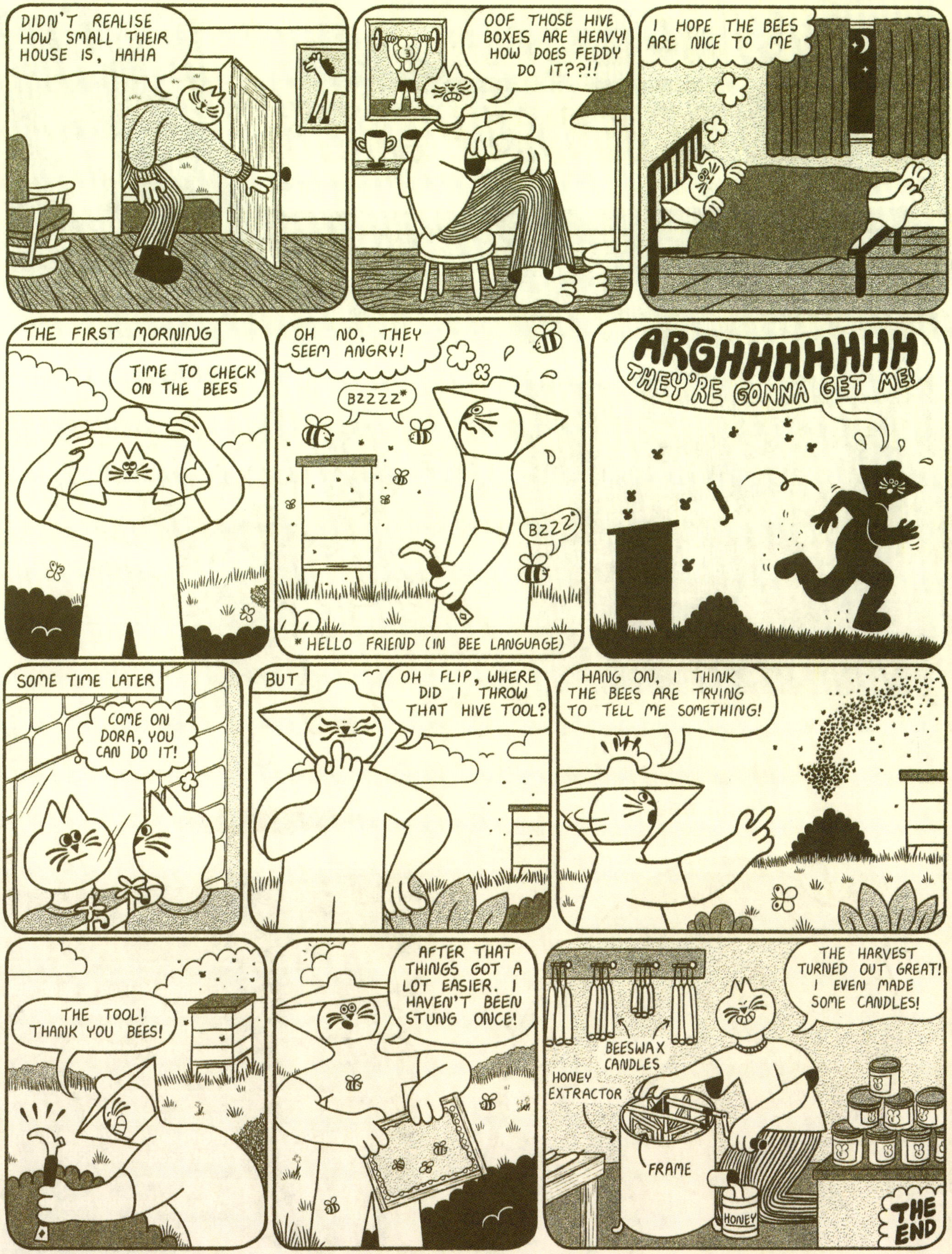
DIDN'T REALISE HOW SMALL THEIR HOUSE IS, HAHA
OOF THOSE HIVE BOXES ARE HEAVY! HOW DOES FEDDY DO IT??!!
I HOPE THE BEES ARE NICE TO ME
THE FIRST MORNING
TIME TO CHECK ON THE BEES
OH NO, THEY SEEM ANGRY!
BZZZZ*
BZZZ
* HELLO FRIEND (IN BEE LANGUAGE)
ARGHHHHHHH
THEY'RE GONNA GET ME!
SOME TIME LATER
COME ON DORA, YOU CAN DO IT!
BUT
OH FLIP, WHERE DID I THROW THAT HIVE TOOL?
HANG ON, I THINK THE BEES ARE TRYING TO TELL ME SOMETHING!
THE TOOL! THANK YOU BEES!
AFTER THAT THINGS GOT A LOT EASIER. I HAVEN'T BEEN STUNG ONCE!
THE HARVEST TURNED OUT GREAT! I EVEN MADE SOME CANDLES!
BEESWAX CANDLES
HONEY EXTRACTOR
FRAME
HONEY
THE END

Dungeons & Dragonflies

BY AARON BAGLEY

ART BY ANDY CHOU MUSSER

IT'S A BUG EAT BUG WORLD! THE ECOLOGICAL BALANCE OF THE MATERIAL PLANE RESTS ON THE THORAX OF THE BRAVEST OF INSECTS IN THIS NEW TABLETOP ROLE-PLAYING GAME. PICK YOUR BUG CHARACTER AND TRAVERSE THE MICRO WORLD OF INSECTUM TO MAINTAIN HARMONY BETWEEN THE PLANT AND ANIMAL KINGDOMS!

| QUOTE | "Good luck to you my insectoid adventurers! I hope you roll gnat-ural 20's!" |

DUNGEON MASTER
The Dragonfly

FAMILY Anisoptera

DECOMPOSER
Dung Beetle

FAMILY Scarabaoeidea

PROFICIENCIES	Strength! Moving a dung ball requires serious muscle. Thus, the Dung Beetle Decomposer can move over 1,000 times its weight!
ABILITIES	Decomposers sustain soil health by recycling nutrients (that's code for poop).
QUOTE	"The Oath of the Poo Ball really stinks, but it's a noble path."

FIGHTER
Ladybug
FAMILY Coccinellidae

PROFICIENCIES	Natural red and black poisonous armor.
ABILITIES	Tactical takedown of garden pests (aphids, mites, scale) which make them great hired mercenaries for preventing harmful infestation.
QUOTE	"I can turn any bush into an ambush!"

POLLINATOR
Butterfly
FAMILY Lepidoptera

PROFICIENCIES	Unlike bees, butterflies can see color and are proficient in pollinating wildflowers—essential for maintaining our material plane's biodiversity.
ABILITIES	Despite having weak armor, these pollinators have the mimicry and camouflage ability.
QUOTE	"Float like a butterfly, pollinate like a bee!"

FOOD SOURCE
Grasshopper
FAMILY Caelifera

PROFICIENCIES	Grasshoppers are a unique class of warrior as they are actually not meant to fight—they're just a great source of food for bugs and birds.
ABILITIES	Great jumpers and they have ears on their abdomen.
QUOTE	"Did you say something?"

PROCESS interview—

OUR YOUTH ADVISORS JAKE, LANIYAH, JOSH, AND EVELYN GO BEHIND THE SCENES WITH PETER KUPER TO UNCOVER THE MAKING OF HIS BOOK *INSECTOPOLIS*.

Kuper, age nine, holding a cecropia moth

Q: HOW DID YOU BEGIN YOUR ARTISTIC PATH?

A: I guess I've always been visual and loved picture books, anything by Dr. Seuss and especially *Harold and the Purple Crayon*. I began reading comics at age seven and remained a lifelong fan, but didn't draw much until I was about fifteen. By the end of high school I realized there was nothing I wanted to do more for a job than draw.

Q: HOW DID YOU BEGIN YOUR CAREER AS AN ILLUSTRATOR?

A: I moved to New York from Cleveland when I was eighteen for a job at an animation company working on the film *Raggedy Ann and Andy*. I had few skills but said I'd be willing to paint whatever they needed, to get a start. When I arrived the job disappeared, but I stayed and found work inking outlines of Richie Rich for comics.

Later, I worked for another artist as his (lowly) assistant. It had very little pay but it was good experience. I still had limited skills so I enrolled in art school and got a much broader understanding of art. Comics still interested me the most, but I had moved on from superhero tales to more personal stories.

Q: DID ANY SPECIFIC JOBS HELP YOU GAIN SKILLS THAT PROVED USEFUL IN THE MAKING OF BOOKS?

A: I have adapted several classic books—Upton Sinclair's *The Jungle*, Franz Kafka's *The Metamorphosis* and most recently *Heart of Darkness* by Joseph Conrad. Spending so much time examining other writers' work and dissecting it to create these adaptations helped me think about my own writing and storytelling in new ways.

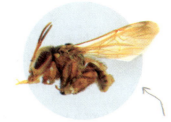

Entomologist MICHAEL S. ENGEL discovered this species of bee and named it SCAPTOTRIGONA KUPERI in honor of Kuper

INSECTOPOLIS
A Natural History
PETER KUPER

Q: What are the steps you took, from creating art in your sketchbook to going professional?

A: I tried lots of different materials, not sticking to one style. I tried printmaking, watercolor, and collage. I played with stencils and spray paint and applied that to comics and graphic novels. I also was concerned about what was happening in the world, so I found subjects based on current events—especially environmental problems.

I pitched myself as not just a style but as a thinker. I could put myself into the work 100% if it was a subject that mattered to me, and that helped me find work where I could do my best job.

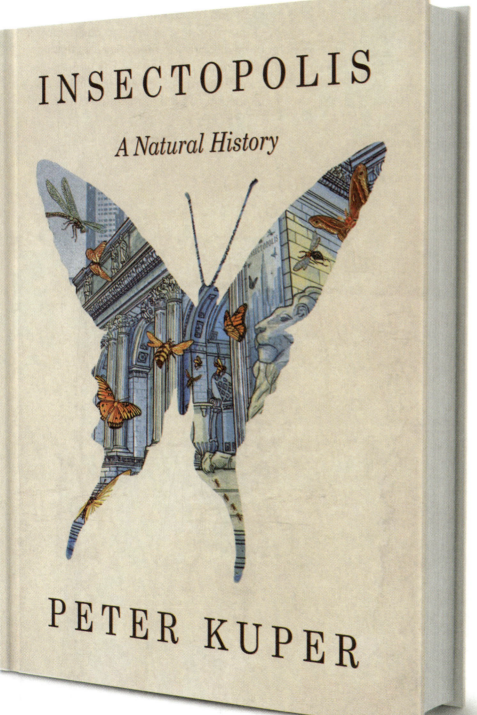

Q: WHERE DID YOU TRAVEL TO DO THE RESEARCH FOR *INSECTOPOLIS*?

A: Mexico, where I lived in 2006–2008 with my wife and daughter. We visited the monarch reserve, which gave me the opportunity to do lots of insect drawings in my sketchbook. It inspired two books: *Diario de Oaxaca*, my collected sketchbooks, and *Ruins*, a fictional account of our time there with a big focus on the monarch's migration.

I had a fellowship at the New York Public Library during Covid-19 and the library not only gave me a tremendous resource for my research, it also presented me with a backdrop for my entire story. It was closed to the public, so it was like being alone in a beautiful museum.

Q: WHAT RESEARCH DID YOU DO WHERE YOU LIVE?

A: I was in Upstate New York, where there are lots of cicadas during the summer. Listening to them make their hundred-decibel mating call helped me sketch out my chapter on them. Fireflies flashing at night, dragonflies and damselflies flitting around a lake, all that inspired details in my book. It's very important to be in nature to have that—but I still LOVE New York City!

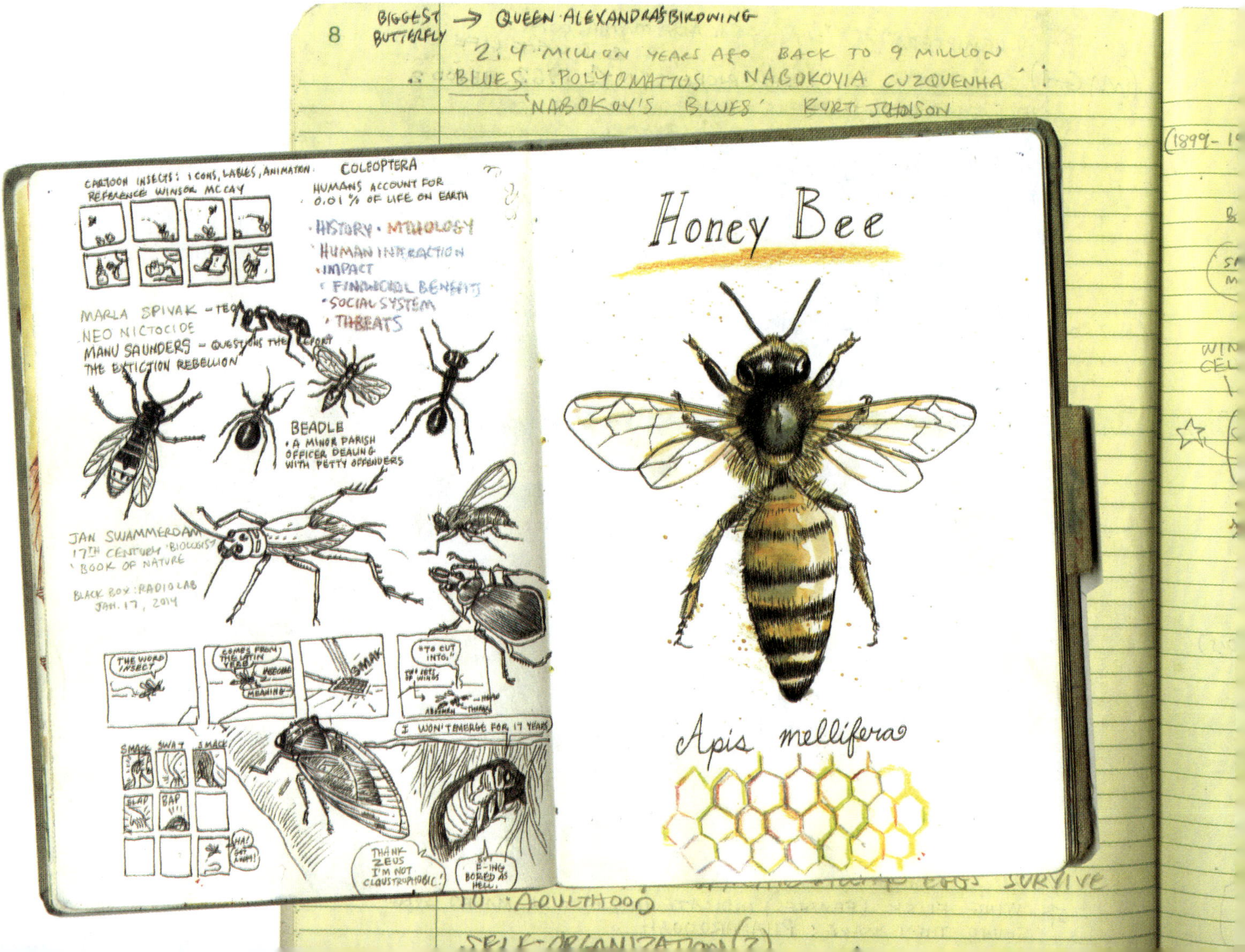

BIGGEST BUTTERFLY → QUEEN ALEXANDRA'S BIRDWING
COLEOPTERA
HUMANS ACCOUNT FOR 0.01% OF LIFE ON EARTH
HISTORY • MYTHOLOGY
HUMAN INTERACTION
IMPACT
FINANCIAL BENEFITS
SOCIAL SYSTEM
THREATS
MARLA SPIVAK
BEADLE
A MINOR PARISH OFFICER DEALING WITH PETTY OFFENDERS
JAN SWAMMERDAM
I WON'T EMERGE FOR 17 YEARS
THANK ZEUS I'M NOT CLAUSTROPHOBIC!
Honey Bee
Apis mellifera

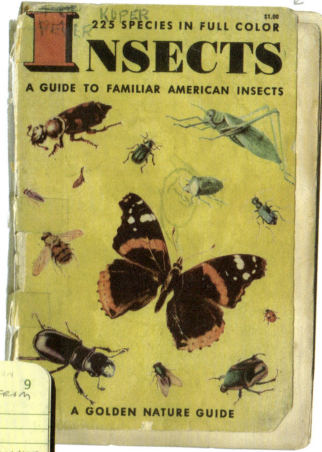

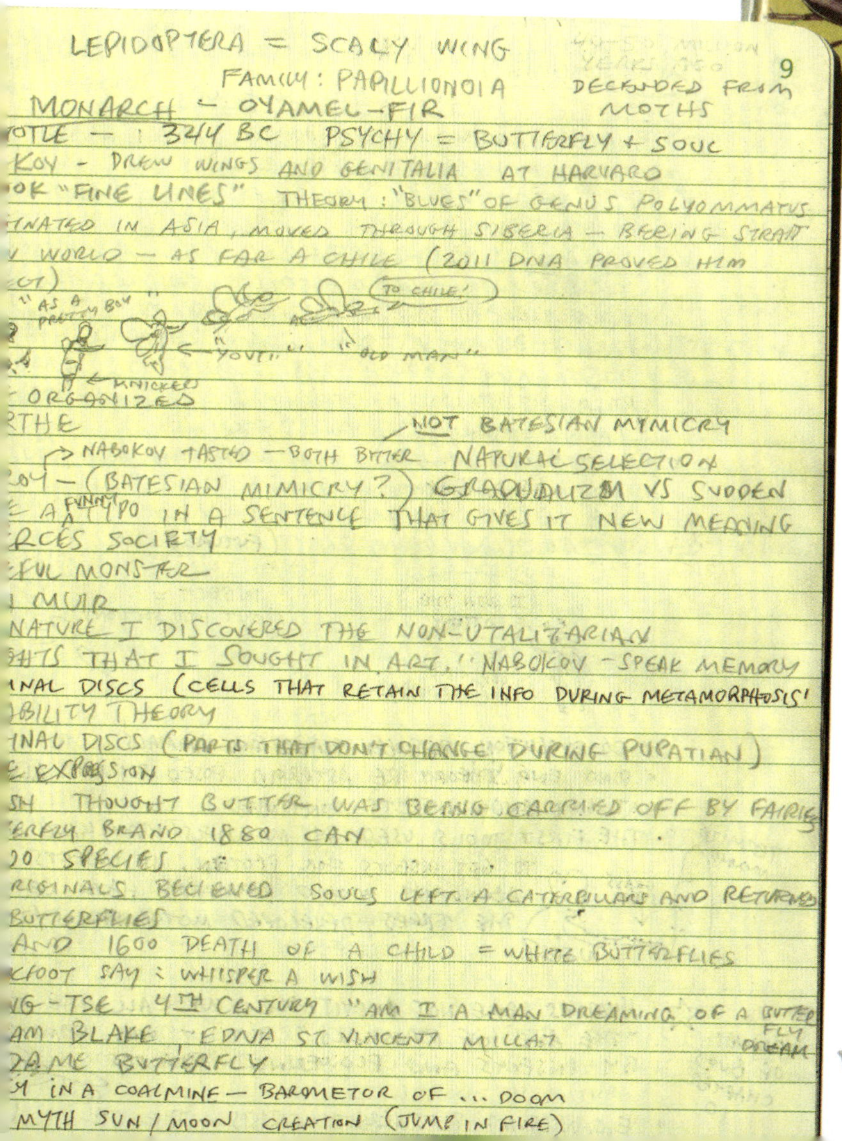

Kuper's first insect book, at age four

KUPER
$1.00
225 SPECIES IN FULL COLOR
INSECTS
A GUIDE TO FAMILIAR AMERICAN INSECTS
A GOLDEN NATURE GUIDE

Q: HOW DID YOU CREATE THE ARTWORK FOR THE ILLUSTRATIONS?

A: I read about the subjects and made notes, then sketched out very rough page layouts. Each chapter was focused on a particular insect, and I collected photo references for each page. I assembled each page in Photoshop, stretching the photos or combining different ones to get everything just as I wanted them. I printed this out, and then light boxed from the photocopies and inked straight onto paper. This made it possible to do all that architectural detail. If I had to pencil and then ink, it would have taken me another year or two. As it was, it took almost five years to complete.

LEPIDOPTERA = SCALY WING
FAMILY: PAPILLIONOIA
9
MONARCH – OYAMEL-FIR
PSYCHY = BUTTERFLY + SOUL
DREW WINGS AND GENITALIA AT HARVARD
"FINE LINES" THEORY: "BLUES" OF GENUS POLYOMMATUS
MOVED THROUGH SIBERIA – BERING STRAIT
AS FAR A CHILE (2011 DNA PROVED HIM
NOT BATESIAN MYMICRY
NABOKOV TASTED – BOTH BITTER
NATURAL SELECTION
(BATESIAN MIMICRY?) GRADUALIZM VS SUDDEN
IN A SENTENCE THAT GIVES IT NEW MEANING
THOUGHT BUTTER WAS BEING CARRIED OFF BY FAIRIES
AND 1600 DEATH OF A CHILD = WHITE BUTTERFLIES
IN A COALMINE – BAROMETOR OF ... DOOM
MYTH SUN / MOON CREATION (JUMP IN FIRE)

sketchbook and development notes for INSECTOPOLIS.

Q: CAN YOU DESCRIBE THE STEPS INVOLVED, FROM IDEA FOR THE BOOK TO THE FINAL PUBLISHED WORK?

A: I had the idea based on an article I read in *The New York Times Magazine* on the insect apocalypse, and also Rachel Carson's *Silent Spring* and Elizabeth Kolbert's *The Sixth Extinction*. I proposed the idea of an insect history for the NY Library's Cullman Fellowship and was fortunate enough to get that. A huge good luck moment was when at the end of the Cullman, I was asked if I wanted to have an exhibition at the library of the work I had done during the fellowship. This pushed me to color more work and form it into a proposal that my agent could pitch to publishers.

WHAT WAS THE FACT-CHECKING PROCESS LIKE BEHIND THE SCENES? DID ANYONE ELSE HELP?

I was very careful to show each chapter to a number of people. I discovered entomologists are like comic book fans—if you are interested in insects, they are happy to talk to you. I managed to contact the top experts for each insect I covered; the fly expert in England, the bee expert in Kansas, the cochineal expert in Mexico, the ant expert in Brooklyn. They all gave me helpful notes. I found people at the Natural History Museum in New York City who let me photograph their insect collections. I wanted as much input as I could get—once the book is published, it's impossible to fix mistakes!

WHAT DO YOU DO ABOUT ARTISTIC OR WRITING BLOCKS?

I recommend copying other artists. The first assignment I give in class is having students copy a full page of another cartoonist's work—not tracing, just by eye. Drawing from a photo you just took or pointless doodling are other ways to unblock. For me, drawing is like exercising. If I do it regularly, then my body craves exercise. The same is true with drawing. Do it regularly and you'll miss it if you don't. Also, I get depressed if I don't draw, so I have a good incentive!

DIARIO DE
OAXACA
PETER KUPER
Introducción de Martín Solares
MÉXICO
sextopiso

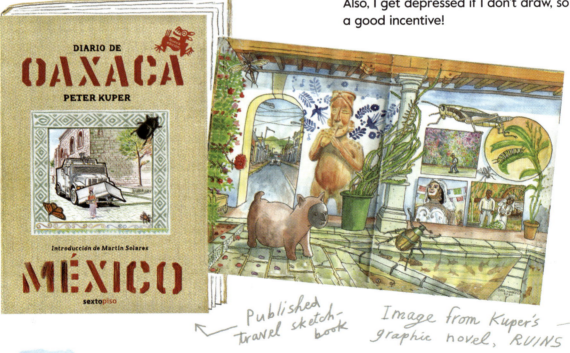

Published travel sketchbook

Image from Kuper's graphic novel, RUINS

IF YOU WERE TO MAKE A BOOK ALL ABOUT JUST ONE INSECT, WHAT WOULD YOU PICK?

The cochineal bug. It produces a gorgeous red color, which is used to dye rugs and fabric. Painters like Vermeer and Van Gogh used it for the red of their paintings. The Spanish found it in Mexico in the 1500s and built their empire on selling it as a dye in Europe—they kept it a secret for over 250 years. There's a book written about this called *The Perfect Red*, which includes espionage and intrigue. I include some of these stories in *Insectopolis*.

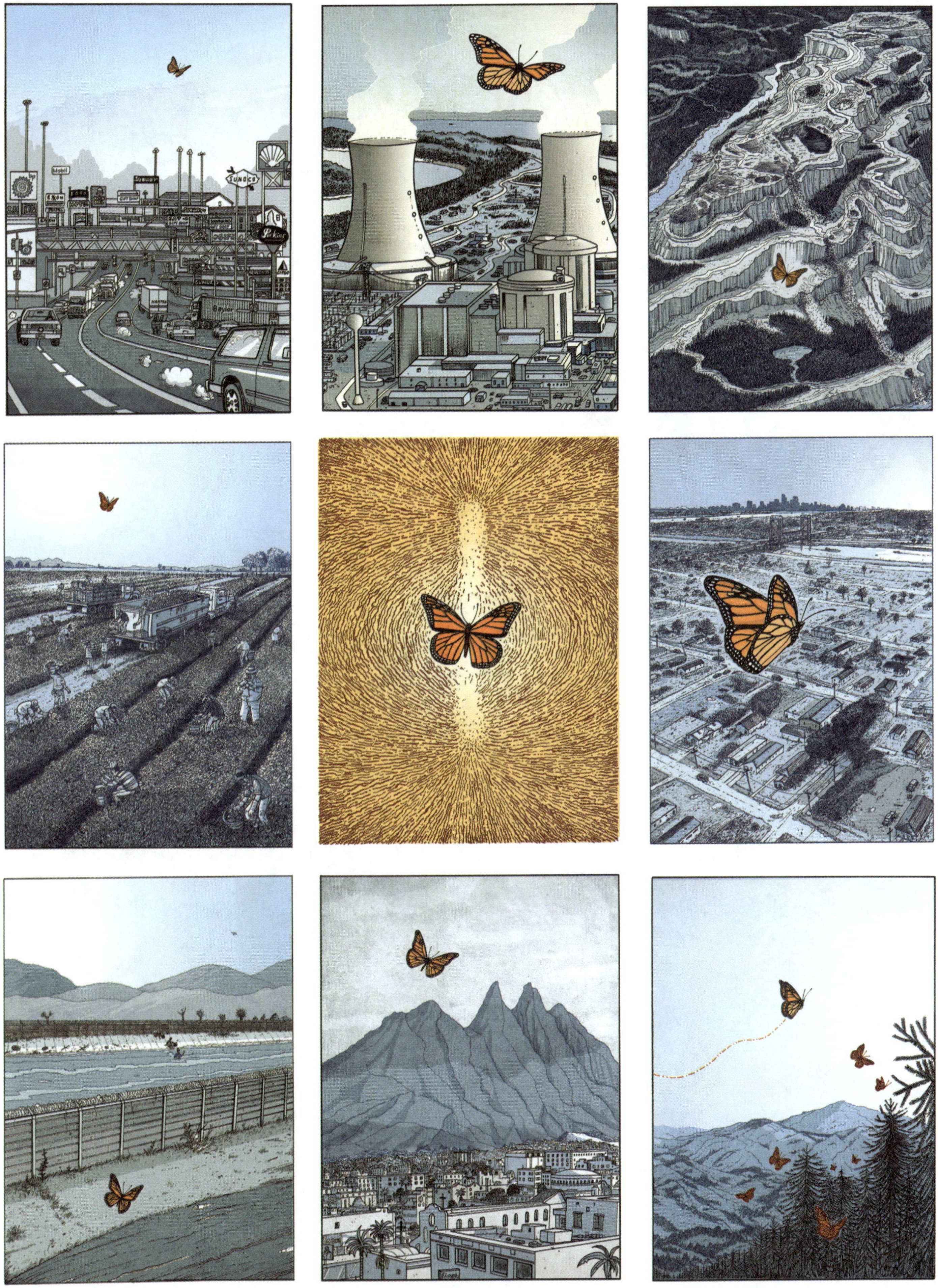
Mobil
EXXON
SUNOCO
Perkins
Baylor

SMALL TALK: FACTOIDS!

CURATED BY LAUREN TAMAKI

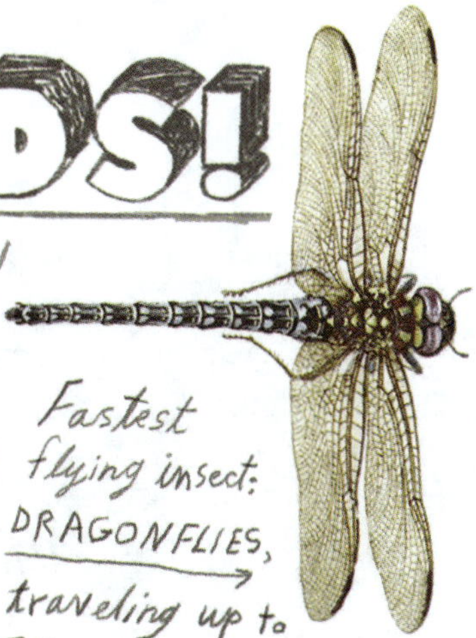

Fastest flying insect: DRAGONFLIES, traveling up to 35 miles per hour.

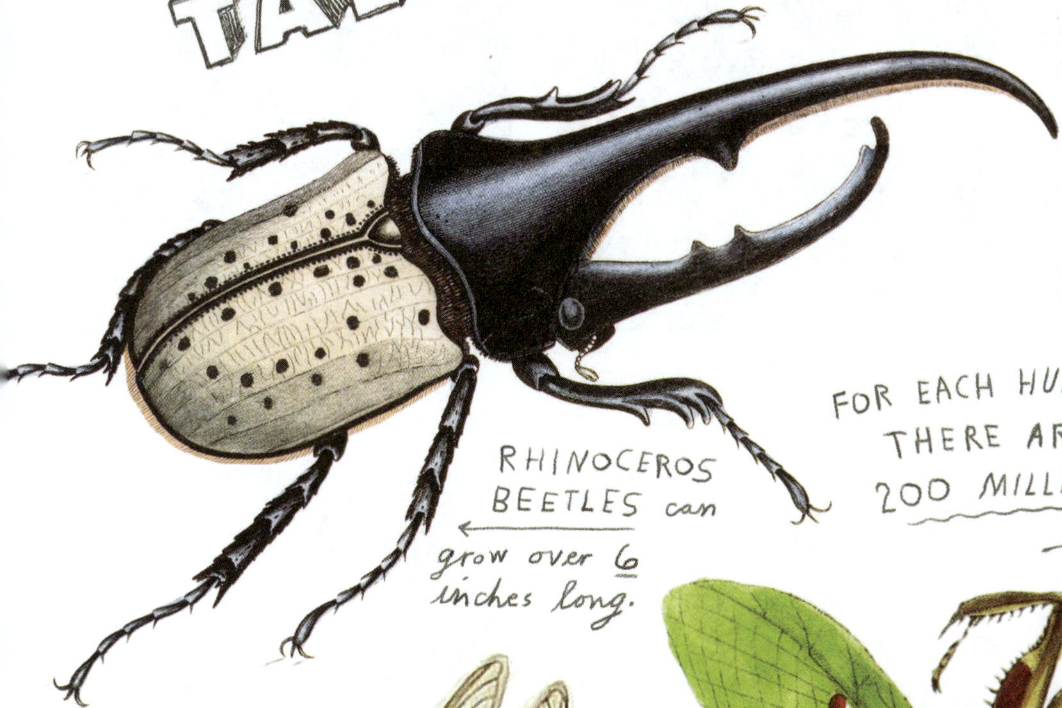

RHINOCEROS BEETLES can grow over 6 inches long.

FOR EACH HUMAN ON THE PLANET, THERE ARE MORE THAN 200 MILLION INSECTS!

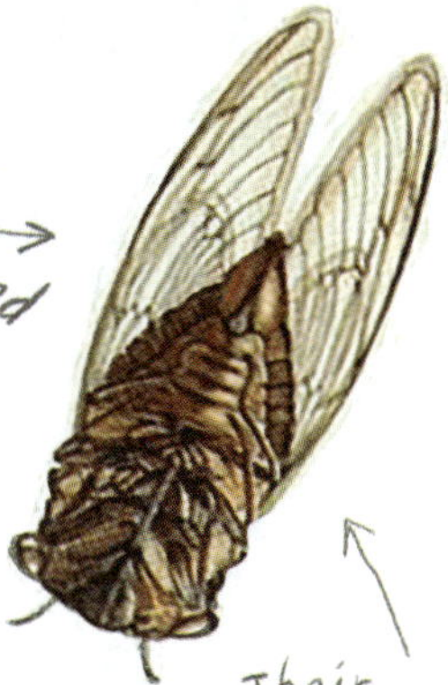

CICADAS are winged insects that live most of their lives underground—for periods of 1, 13, or 17 years.

Their songs reach 120 decibels—which is as loud as a chainsaw.

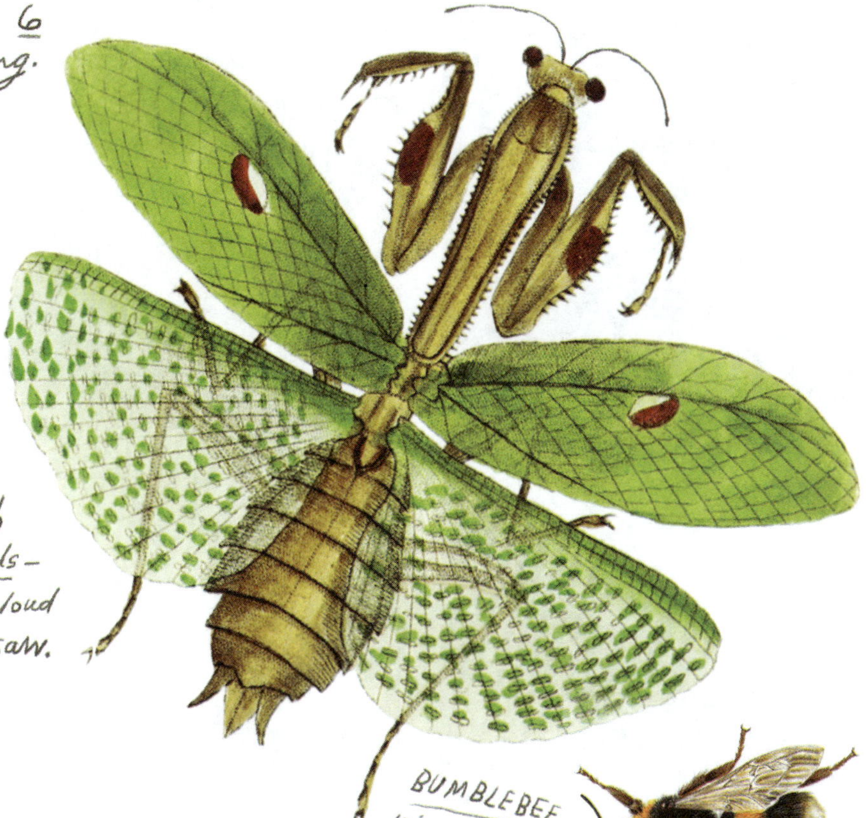

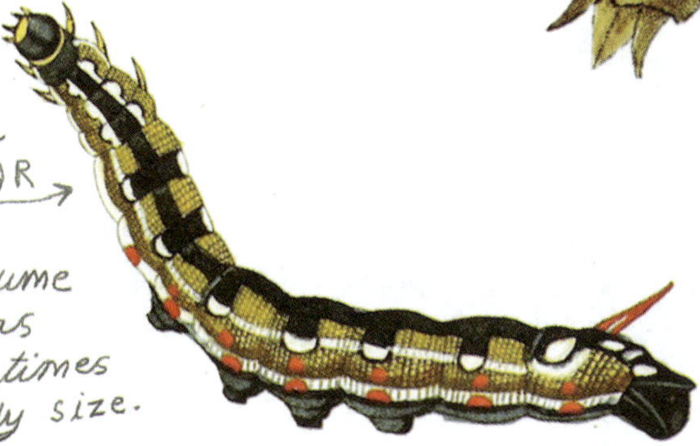

The life purpose of a CATERPILLAR is to eat. They consume as much as 27,000 times their body size.

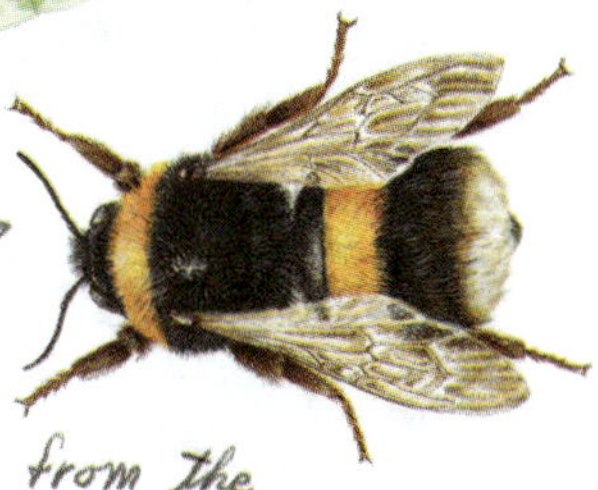

BUMBLEBEE wings beat 130–240 times per second.

The vibrations from the rapid wing movement shake loose pollen from flowers—this is called "BUZZ POLLINATION."

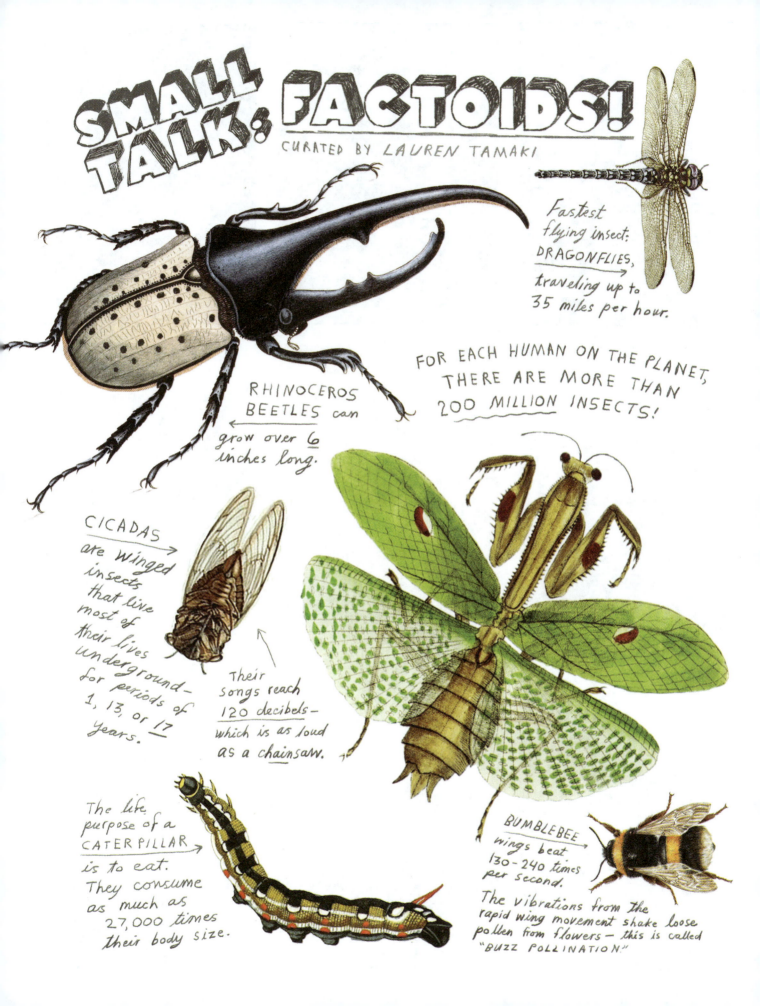

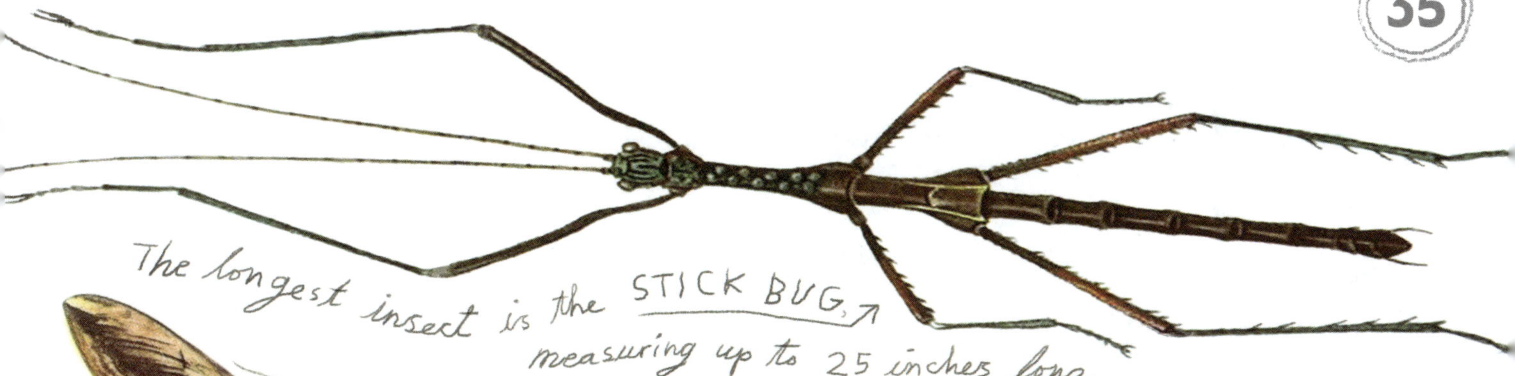

The longest insect is the STICK BUG, measuring up to 25 inches long.

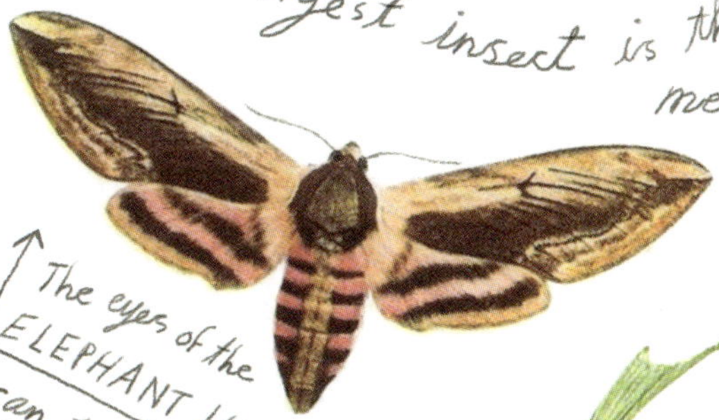

The eyes of the ELEPHANT HAWK MOTH can tell which flowers have the most nectar by color, even in the darkest night.

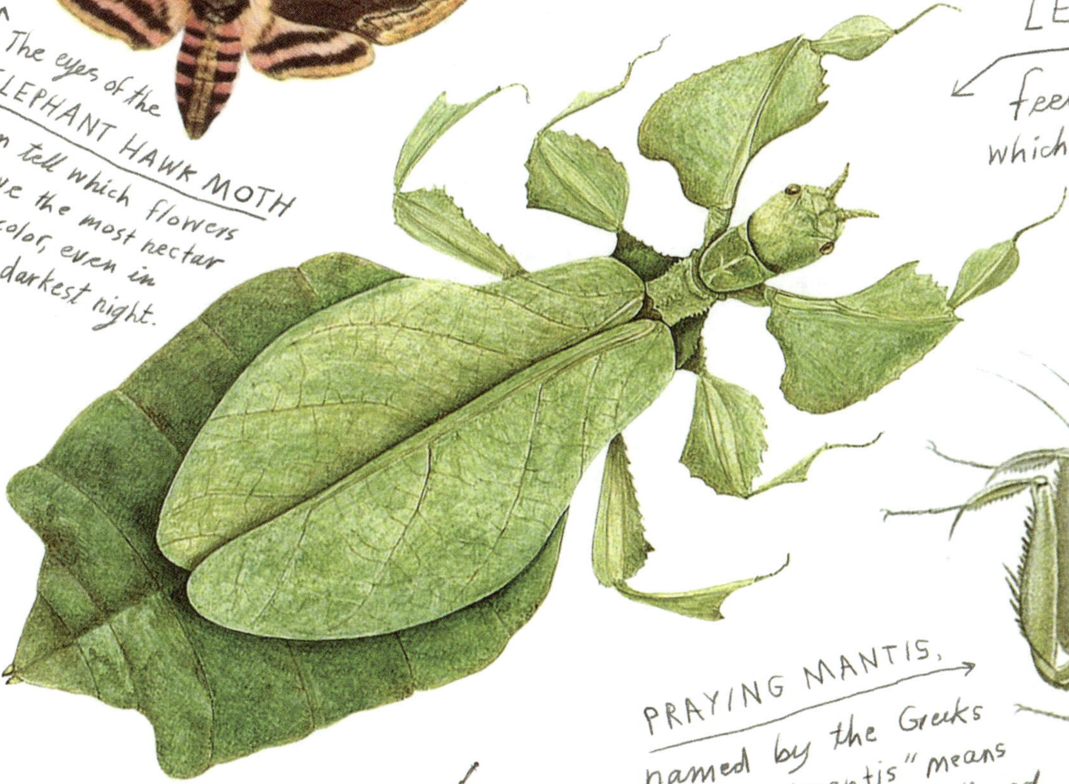

LEAF BUGS feed on leaves, which give them the chlorophyll they need to maintain their green coloration.

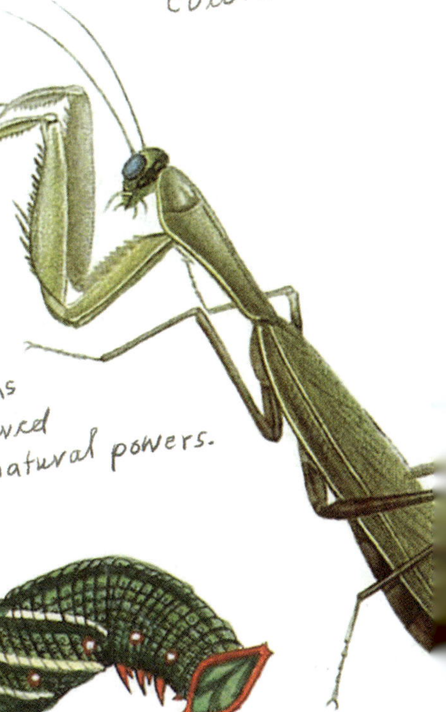

PRAYING MANTIS, named by the Greeks because "mantis" means "diviner," and they believed the insect had supernatural powers.

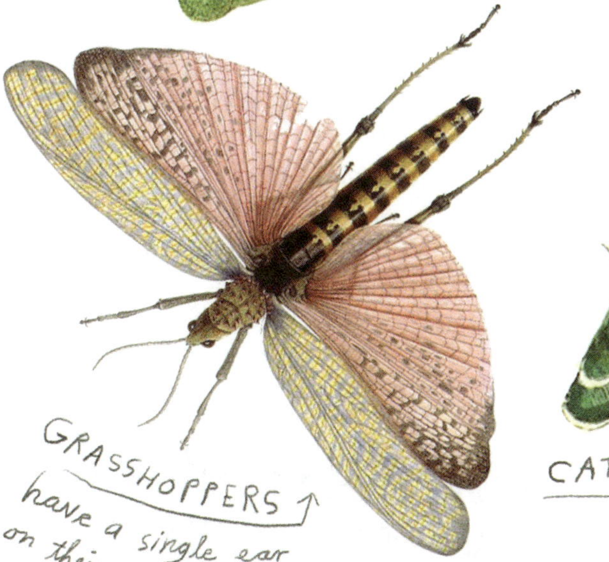

GRASSHOPPERS have a single ear on their bellies.

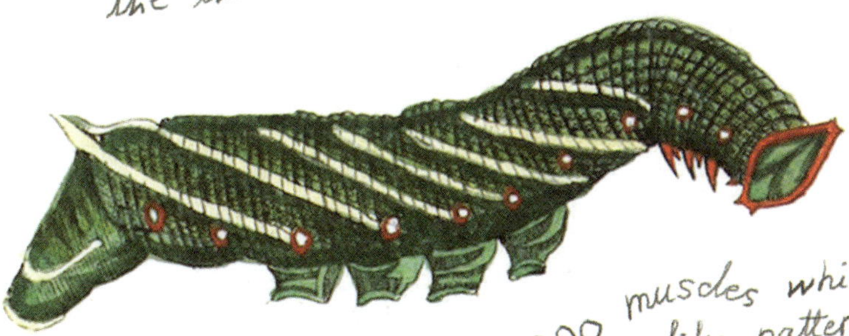

CATERPILLARS have 4,000 muscles which move in a wave-like pattern from back to front. This kind of movement is not found in any other creature on earth.

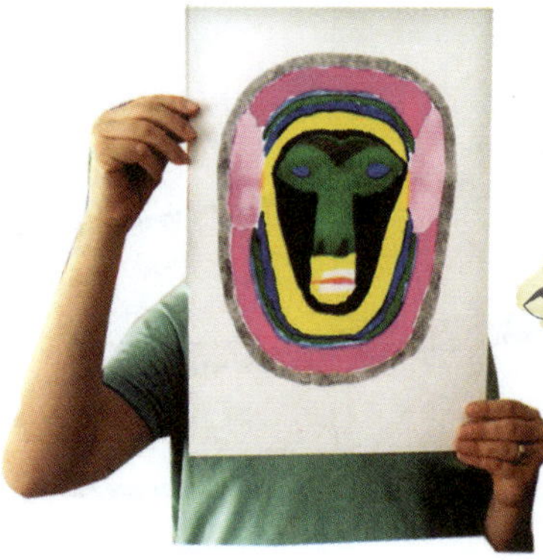

interview:

WITH OUR COVER ARTIST JESÚS CISNEROS

JESÚS HAILS FROM MADRID, SPAIN, WHERE HE WORKS ON BOOKS AND EDITORIAL PROJECTS. HE TRAVELS THE GLOBE, TEACHING WORKSHOPS ABOUT ART.

Tell us about a book from childhood that still influences you today.

I spent hours reading comics with my friends or alone in my room when I was a child. However, the stories I remember most vividly were the classic tales that my little sister and I had in adapted versions (some of the pages are scribbled on with pen by her, so I think she liked them too). I believe that since then, I have never stopped returning to the classics that have deeply influenced me, like Alice's Adventures in Wonderland, *for example. It seems to me like a book where anything is possible.*

On the other hand, some books I would have loved to read as a child but discovered later are the Babar stories by Jean de Brunhoff. The Story of Babar *is a marvelous work that can be enjoyed at any age. The illustrations are delicate, expressive, elegant, and tender. We follow the little elephant on his journey from the jungle to the city, his adventures are both everyday and fantastic, with touches of melancholy and humor. The book is an eternal classic, a hot-air balloon that takes us back to childhood.*

Describe an unusual object in your studio.

On a planner, supported by a cardboard base, I keep a small twig. It looks fragile, but it has survived multiple falls and was lost for a few days after a move. When I first saw it during a walk in the park, it seemed like a sculpture made by nature, and I picked it up immediately. It is a wanderer moving forward, cutting through the air with its arms outstretched as if heading to meet someone.

What's up next on your artistic plate?

I would love to paint ceramics again. Last year, I decorated a long series of bowls, an experience that turned out to be very stimulating. A ceramicist shaped the pieces, and I filled them with images of plants and animals. It was a process full of learning and surprises. When the kiln was finally opened, revealing the pieces with their final colors transformed by fire, it was always magical. A celebration. Drawn by the vibrant colors, some curious insects began to arrive with their long legs, antennae, and proboscises, ready to sip the nectar from the strange painted plants.

What did you think you would be when you grew up?

When I was a child, I couldn't picture myself as an adult. I remember that my main (and only) interest was playing. Back then, the kids in my neighborhood and I spent a lot of time outdoors, improvising excursions, adventures that took us into imaginary landscapes. Drawing was also a form of play. And I was always certain that I would never stop making drawings.

What is one of the weirdest jobs you have done in the past? (Doesn't have to be art related.)

For six months, I worked in a metal factory making parts for elevators, especially ceiling light grilles. I wasn't there for a long time, and though it was sometimes tough, it wasn't a terrible experience. At least it was a form of manual labor, and I've always liked that. Sometimes, when I take an elevator, I check how the grilles look! On another occasion, I gave private in-home Latin lessons to students who needed to pass their exams. To be honest, my knowledge of Latin didn't go beyond the basics, but my students managed to pass.

What do you do when you hit a roadblock?

Moments of doubt are common; they are part of the process. Like anyone, I have crises, but they usually help me reconsider the project and approach it from a different

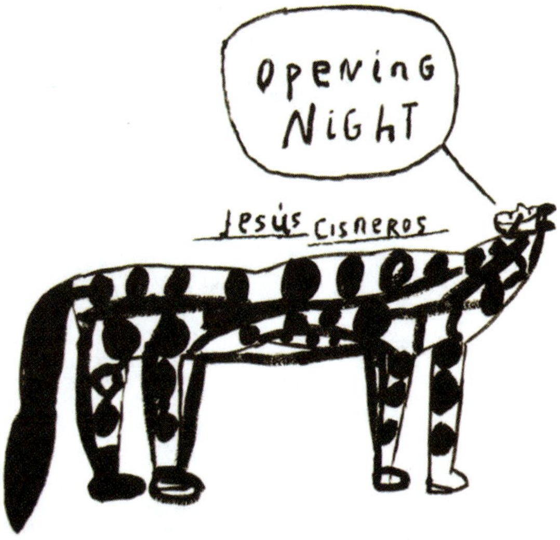
OPENING NIGHT
JESÚS CISNEROS

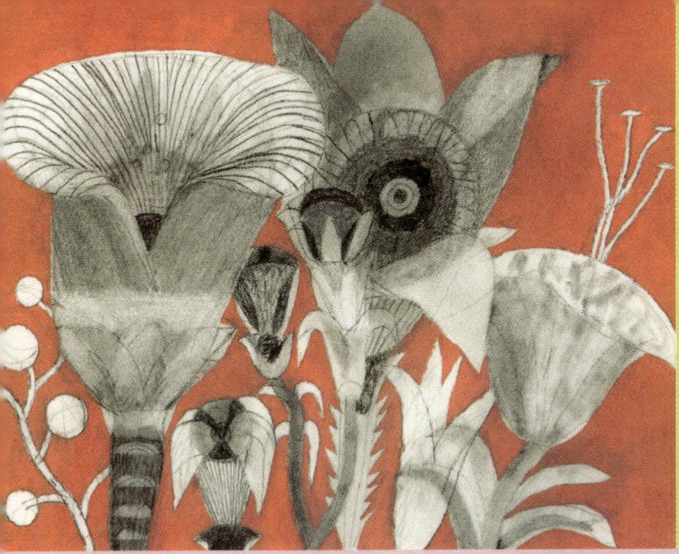

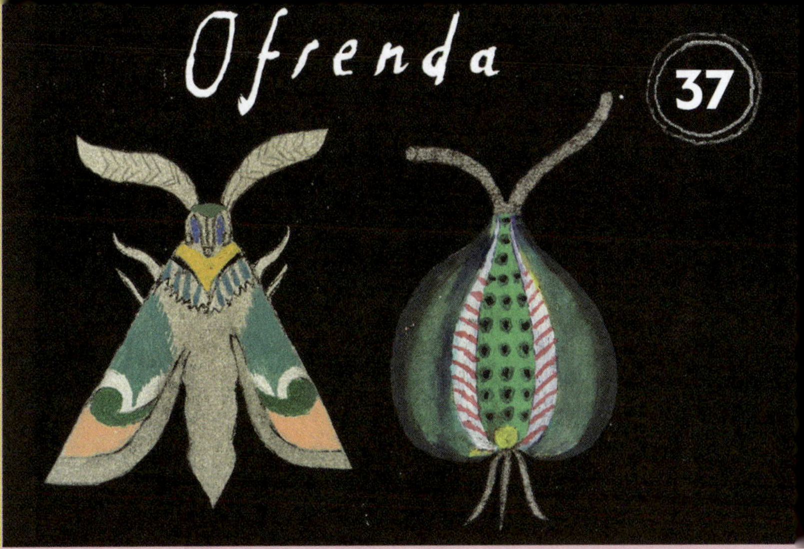
Ofrenda
37

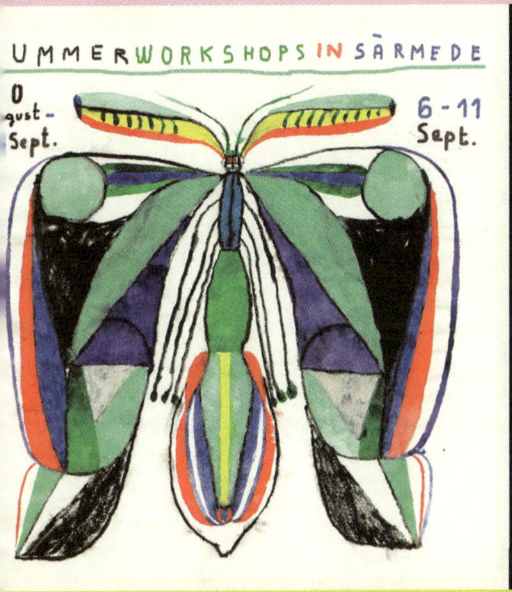
UMMERWORKSHOPS IN SÀRMEDE
0
gust-
Sept.
6-11
Sept.

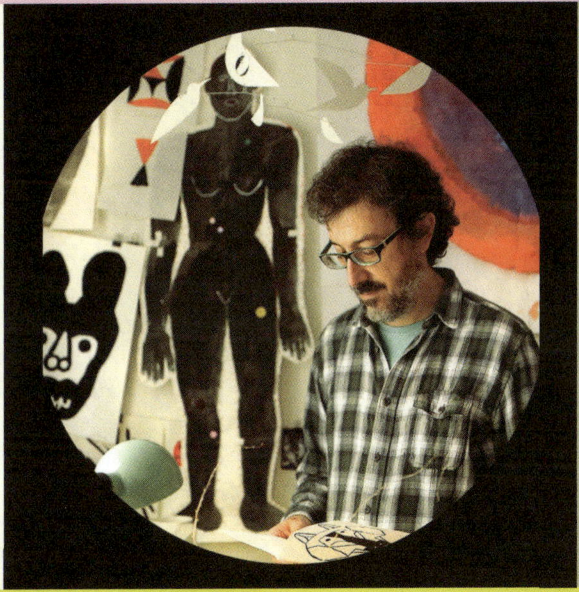

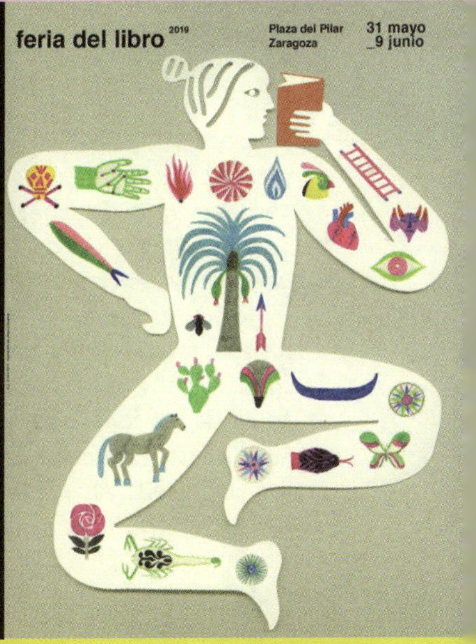
feria del libro 2019
Plaza del Pilar
Zaragoza
31 mayo
_9 junio

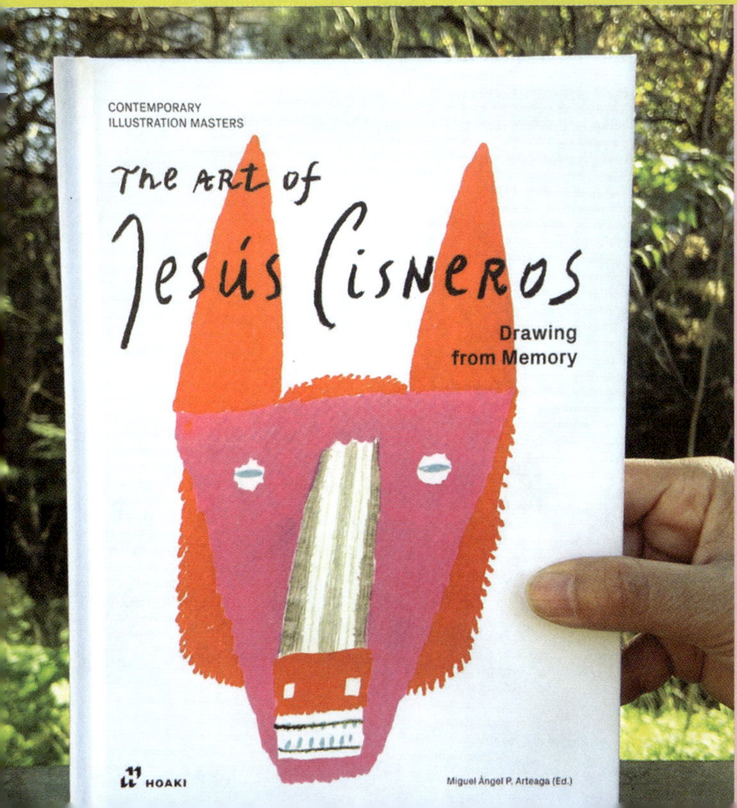
CONTEMPORARY
ILLUSTRATION MASTERS
The Art of
Jesús Cisneros
Drawing
from Memory
HOAKI
Miguel Ángel P. Arteaga (Ed.)

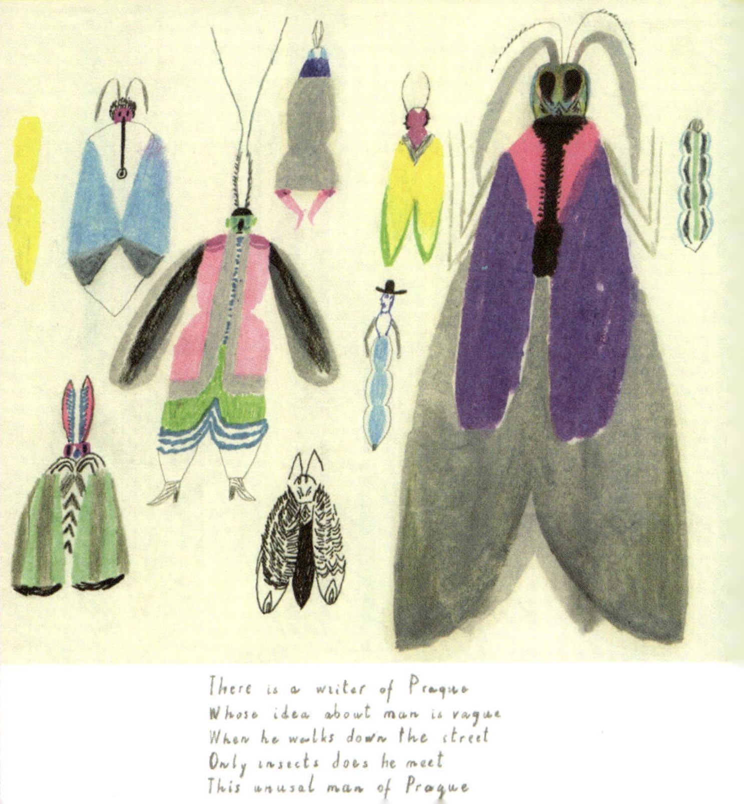
There is a writer of Prague
Whose idea about man is vague
When he walks down the street
Only insects does he meet
This unusual man of Prague

interview, continued

perspective. It's important to accept that what we dislike at a given moment is just a necessary step toward achieving the best result. Some of the drawings or paintings I've felt most satisfied with have come right after a phase of uncertainty.

What's your favorite thing about living in Zaragoza?
Zaragoza is a city where life is peaceful. My favorite spot in the city is the Ebro River. Along its banks, there is a long walkway where I sometimes go for a walk with my wife, feeling embraced by the trees and distanced from the noise of the cars. On the other hand, I travel quite a lot to give workshops around the world, so coming back to a quiet city is always nice.

What would be a future dream project?
Alice's Adventures in Wonderland is a nice challenge for any illustrator. This text navigates between play and unbridled imagination, and I imagine it's possible to think of drawings that keep with this spirit, even more when the illustrations of John Tenniel are already an inseparable reference to this work. These days, while working on the cover for *Illustoria* magazine, I remembered the dialogue with the mosquito in chapter three of *Through the Looking-Glass*. The poor insect whispers bad jokes in Alice's ear and, desolate, sighs and cries bitter tears. Both, then, have a conversation about the advantages of having or not having a name. And later Alice enters the "Forest where things have no name" where she has an unforgettable encounter with a fawn. The text goes from humorous to philosophical with poetry and unparalleled charm.

What is your favorite bug to draw? Is there a bug you dislike strongly (or are scared of!)?
I really like drawing insects, as you know. Real spiders scare me a bit, but my drawn spiders are quite cute. Another insect I really like to draw is grasshoppers, with their fantastic mechanism for propelling themselves and making huge jumps. Although I always forget a bit about the details of their anatomy and have to remember (or invent) them when drawing!

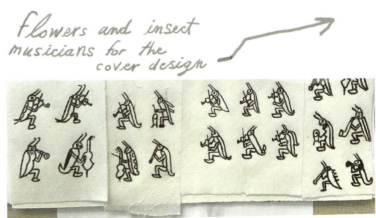

flowers and insect musicians for the cover design

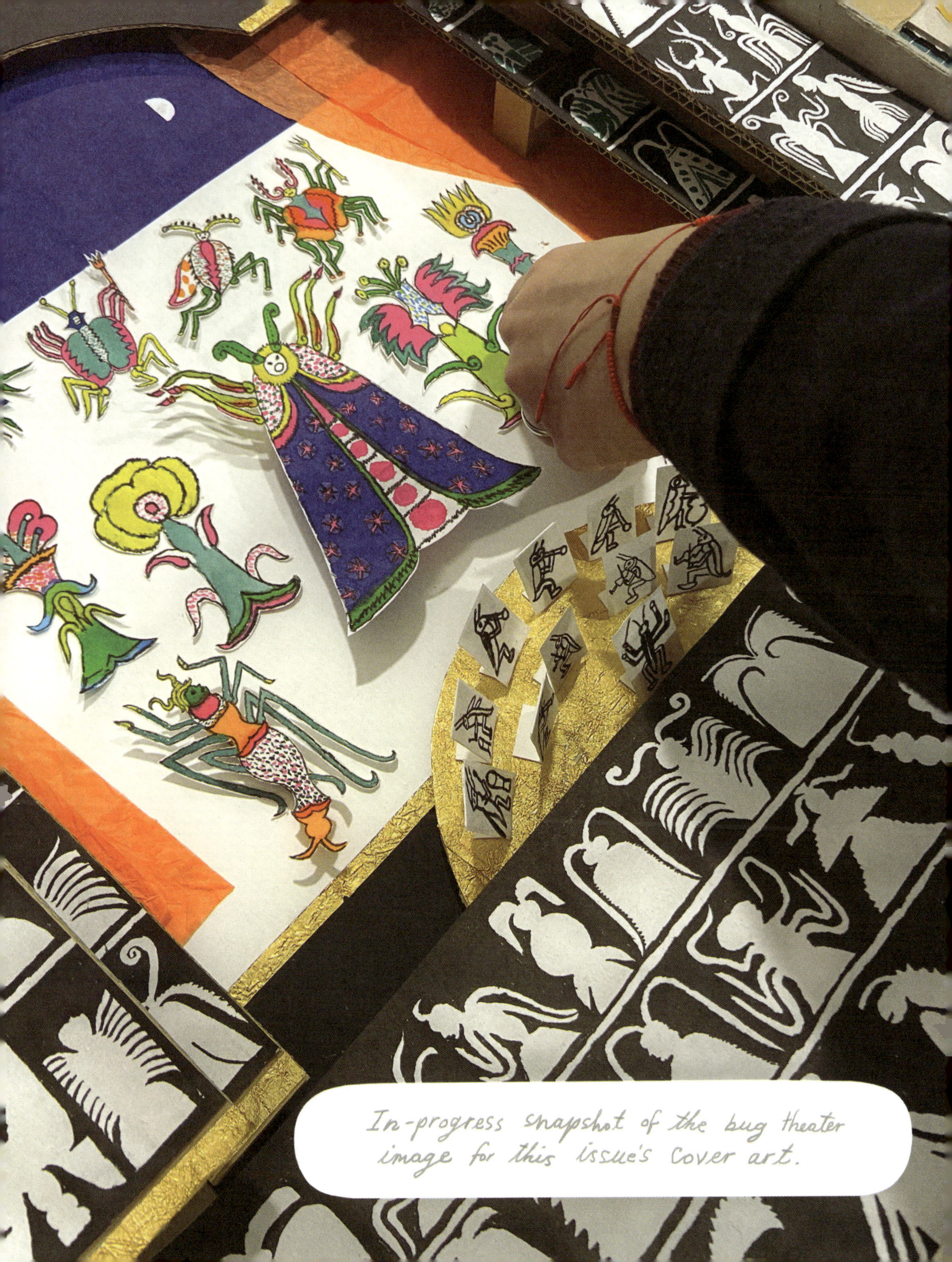

In-progress snapshot of the bug theater image for this issue's cover art.

interview, continued

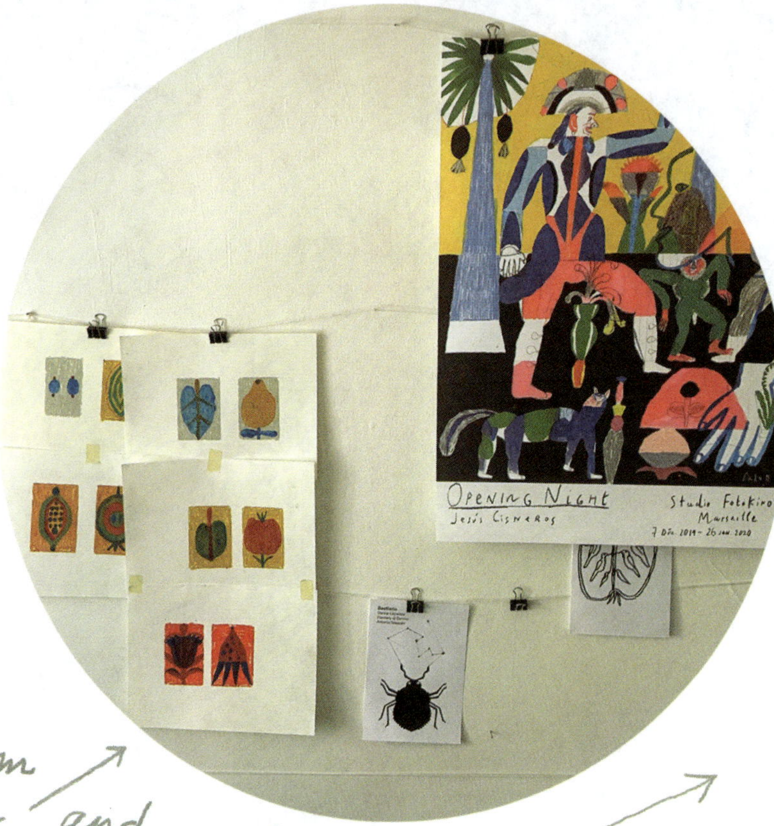
Opening Night
Jesús Cisneros
Studio Fotokino
Marseille
7 Déc. 2019 – 26 Jan. 2020

Favorite snack while working?
Chips.

Album listened to recently.
This Stupid World by Yo La Tengo

scenes from studio and art desk

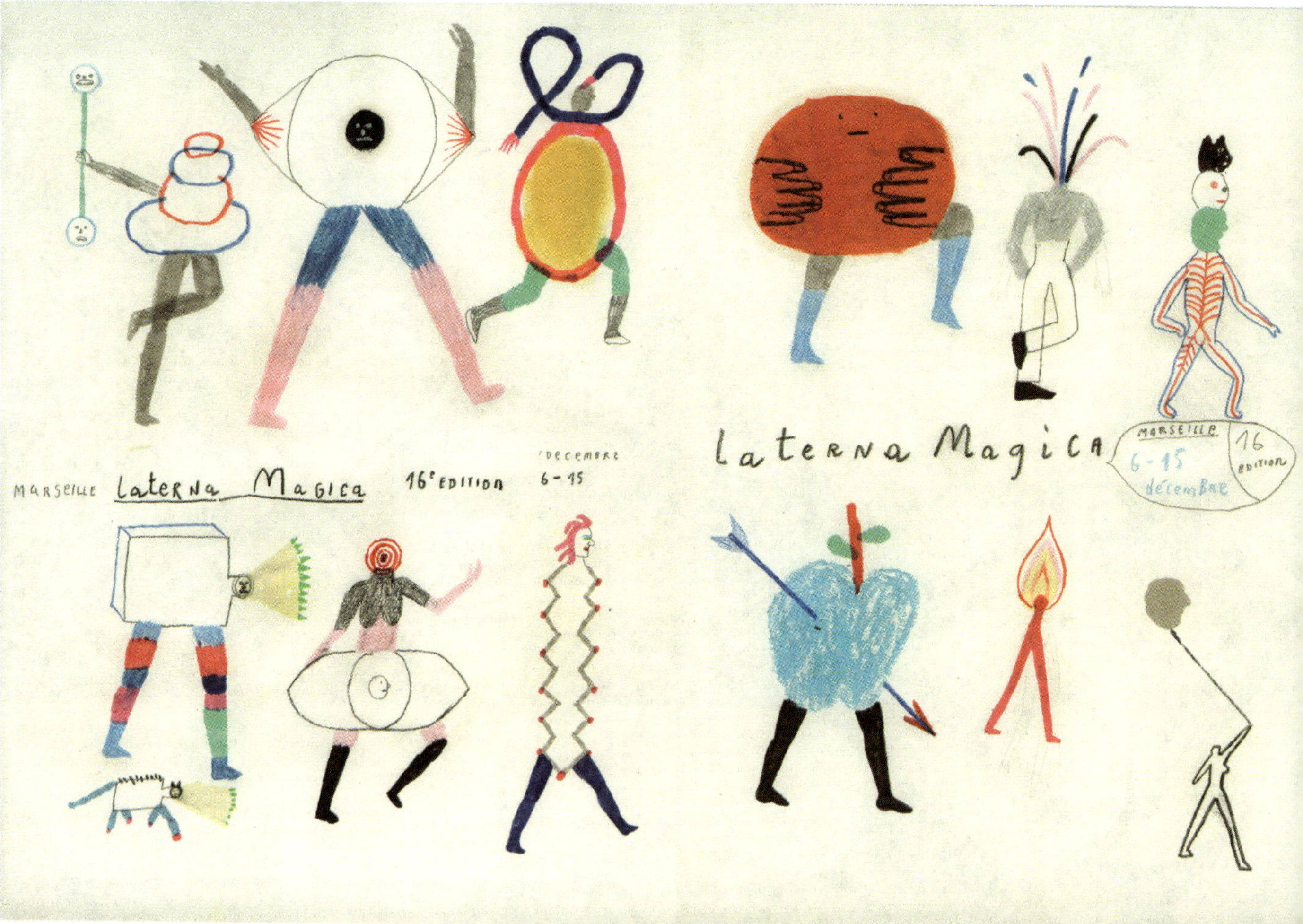
MARSEILLE laterna Magica 16e EDITION
décembre 6-15
laterna Magica
MARSEILLE
6-15
décembre
16
EDITION

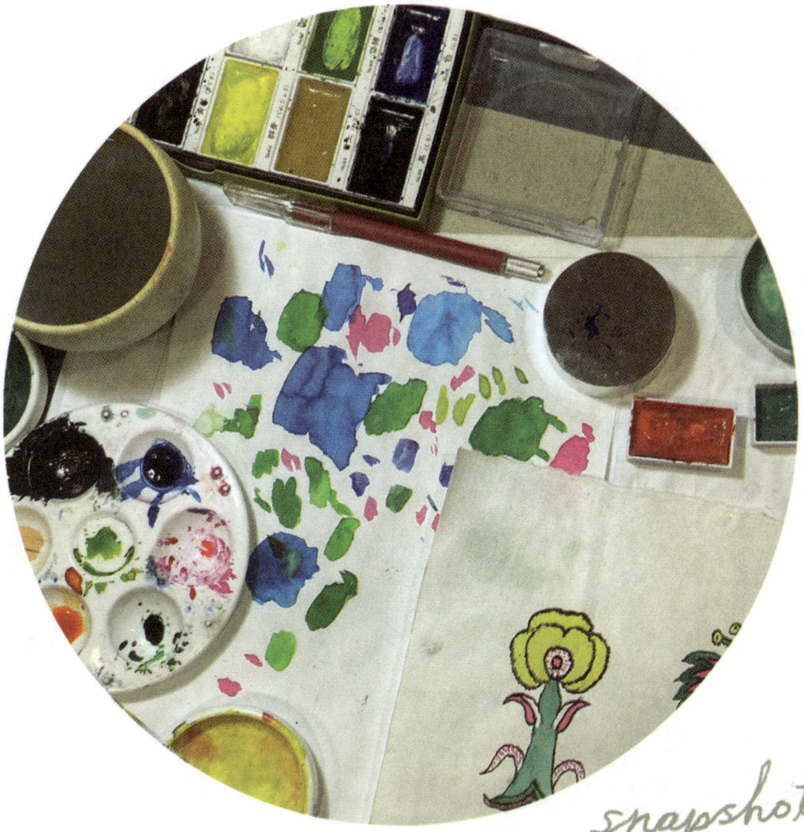

Morning person or night owl?
Morning person.

Art supply you can't live without?
Watercolor graphite.

snapshots of character designs ↓

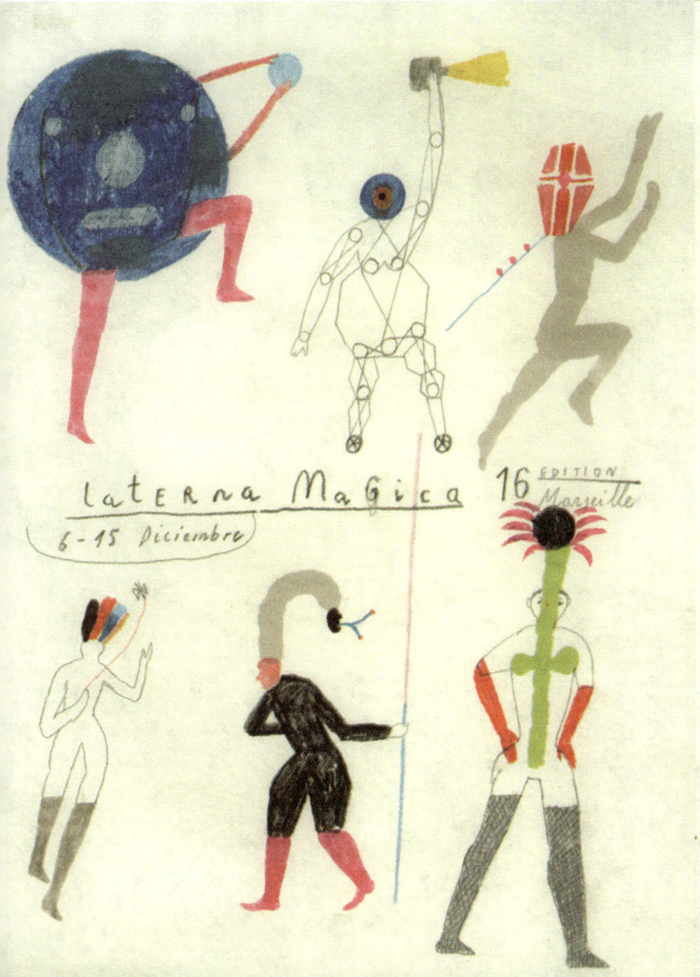
LaterNa MaGica
16 EDITION
Marseille
6-15 Diciembre

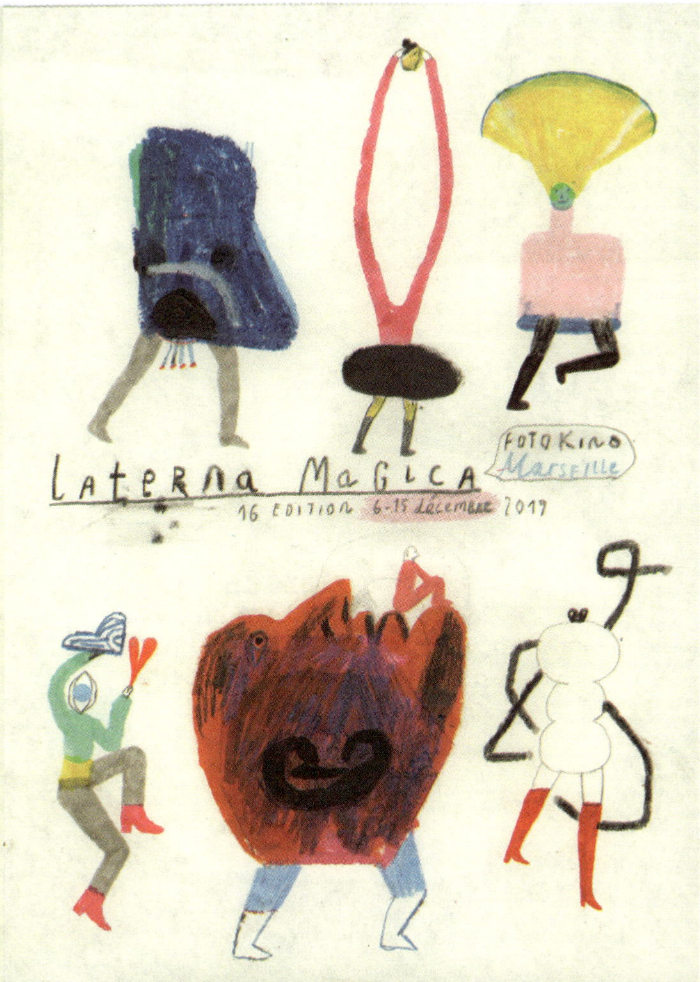
LAterNa MaGICA
FOTOKINO
Marseille
16 EDITION 6-15 décembre 2017

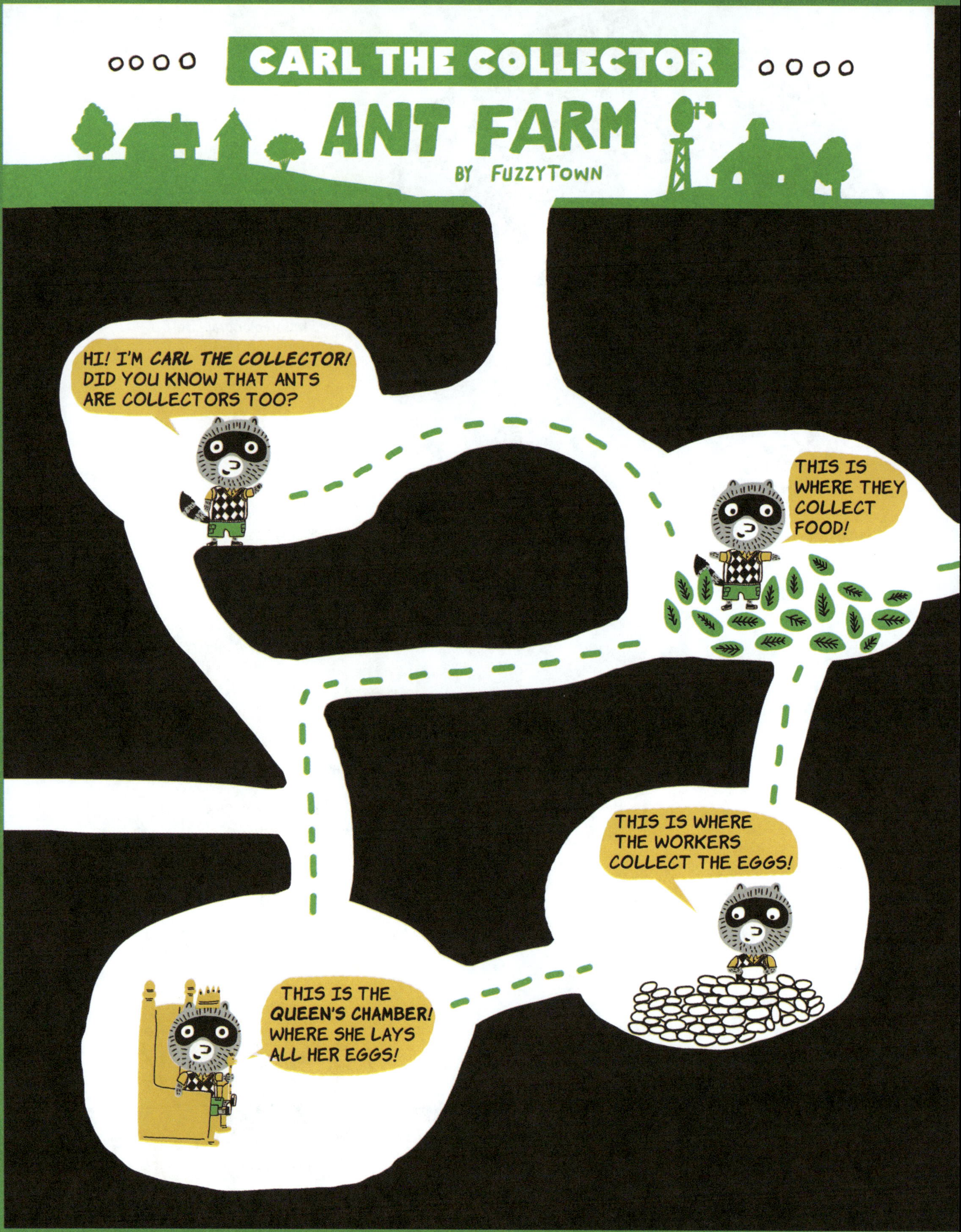
CARL THE COLLECTOR
ANT FARM
BY FUZZYTOWN
HI! I'M CARL THE COLLECTOR! DID YOU KNOW THAT ANTS ARE COLLECTORS TOO?
THIS IS WHERE THEY COLLECT FOOD!
THIS IS WHERE THE WORKERS COLLECT THE EGGS!
THIS IS THE QUEEN'S CHAMBER! WHERE SHE LAYS ALL HER EGGS!

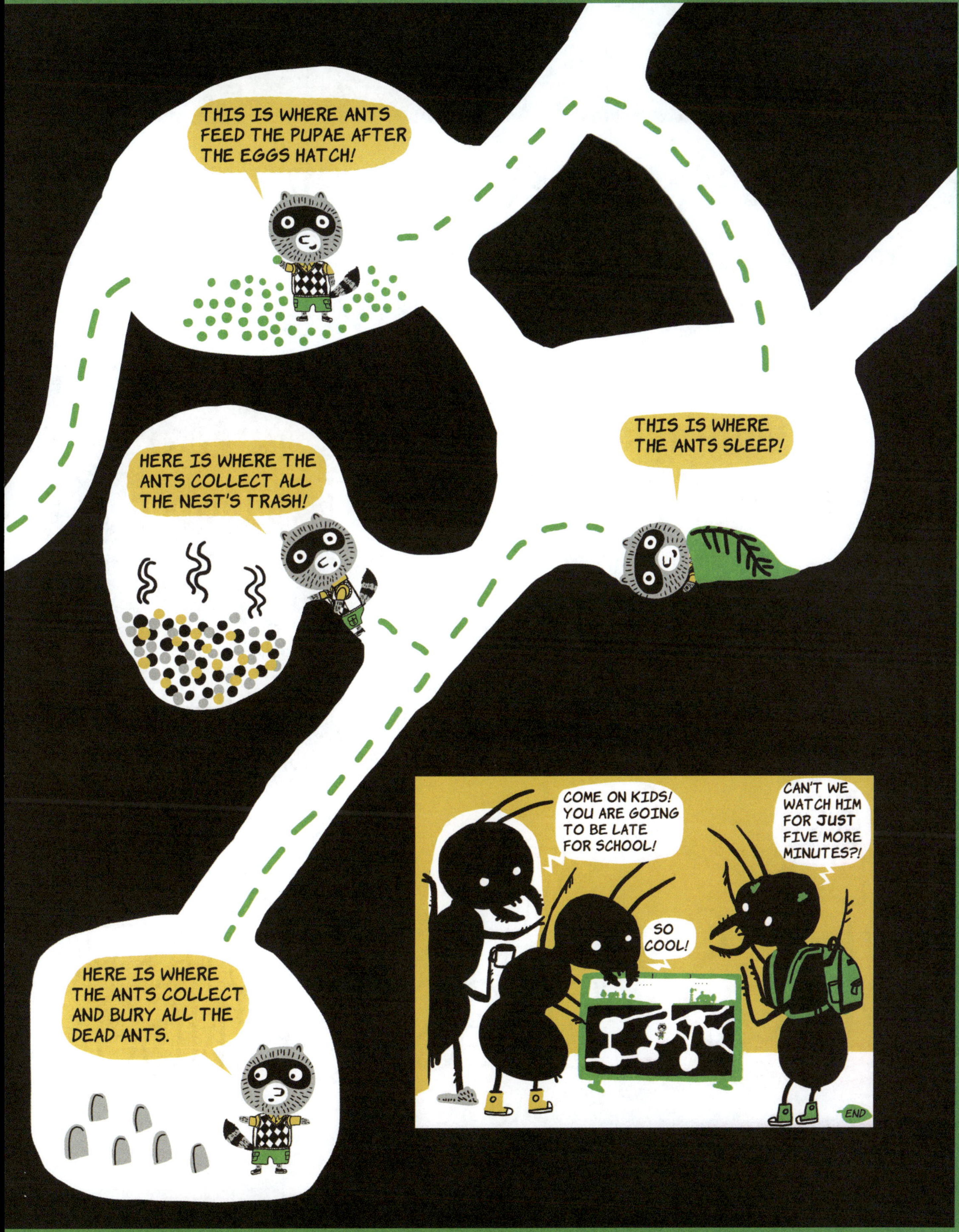
THIS IS WHERE ANTS FEED THE PUPAE AFTER THE EGGS HATCH!
THIS IS WHERE THE ANTS SLEEP!
HERE IS WHERE THE ANTS COLLECT ALL THE NEST'S TRASH!
HERE IS WHERE THE ANTS COLLECT AND BURY ALL THE DEAD ANTS.
COME ON KIDS! YOU ARE GOING TO BE LATE FOR SCHOOL!
CAN'T WE WATCH HIM FOR JUST FIVE MORE MINUTES?!
SO COOL!
END

thames &hudson

BEETLES, BUTTERFLIES, SPIDERS, AND MORE—DISCOVER THE WONDERFUL WORLD OF BUGS!

"Whimsically illustrated"
—*School Library Journal* on *The Big Book of Bugs*

Hardcover • Ages 3+
$24.95

Hardcover • Ages 4+
$19.95

Board book • Ages 0–3
$9.99

Game • Ages 3+
$23.95

thamesandhudsonusa.com | @thamesandhudsonusa | distributed by W.W. Norton & Co.

The only thing better than playing make believe is playing make bee-lieve with your favorite grown up!

A delightful read aloud from Caldecott Honor winner **SHAWN HARRIS**

"Let's be readers and explore this book together—again and again and again."
—Kirkus Reviews

Grab your crayons and head to HolidayHousebooks.com for downloadable activity sheets based on the book!

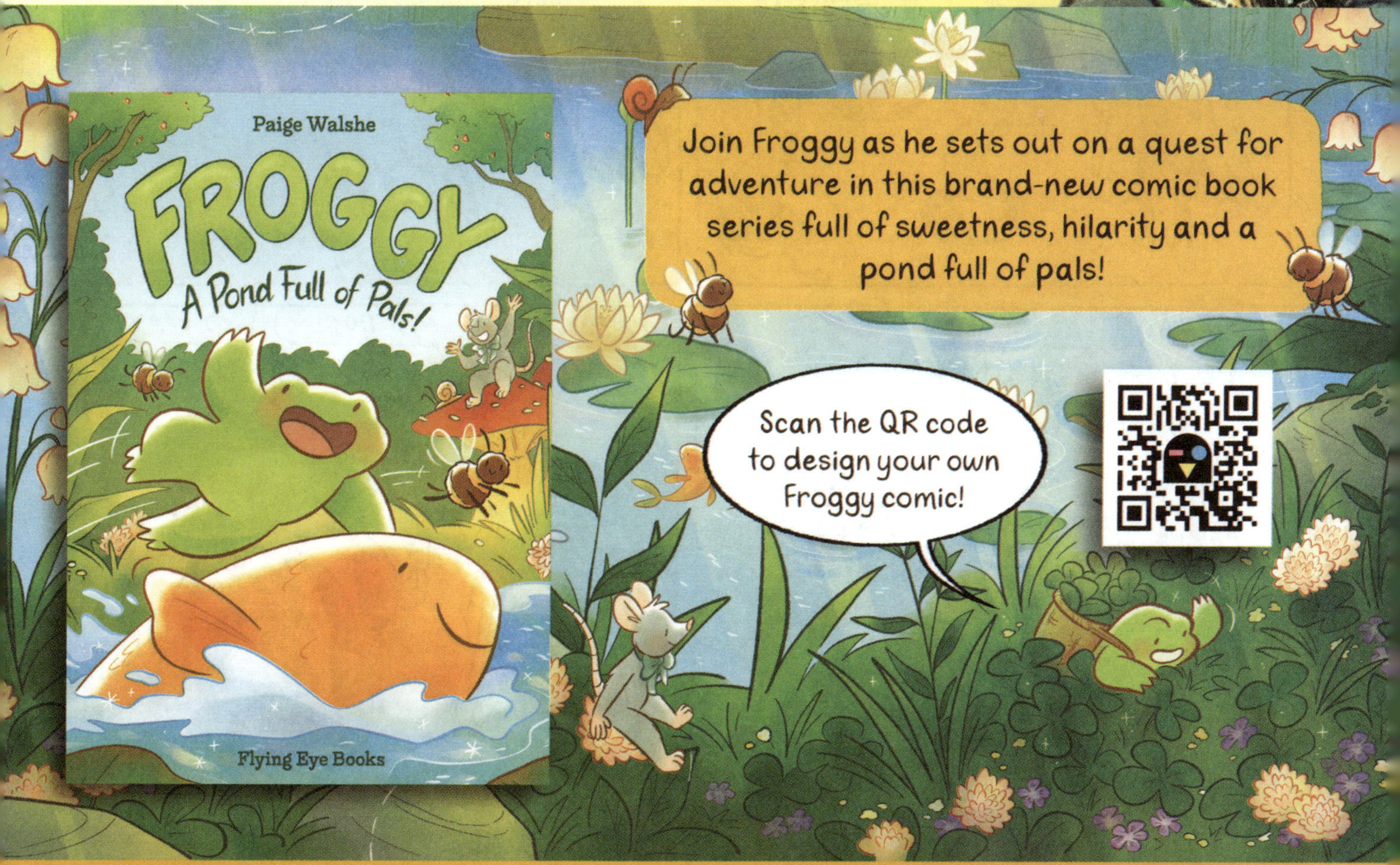

Neal Porter Books • HOLIDAY HOUSE

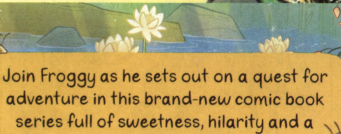

Join Froggy as he sets out on a quest for adventure in this brand-new comic book series full of sweetness, hilarity and a pond full of pals!

Scan the QR code to design your own Froggy comic!

Published by Flying Eye Books | www.flyingeyebooks.com — FLYING EYE BOOKS — @FlyingEyeBooks

CONTINUED ON PAGE 62

KATHARINA KULENKAMPFF

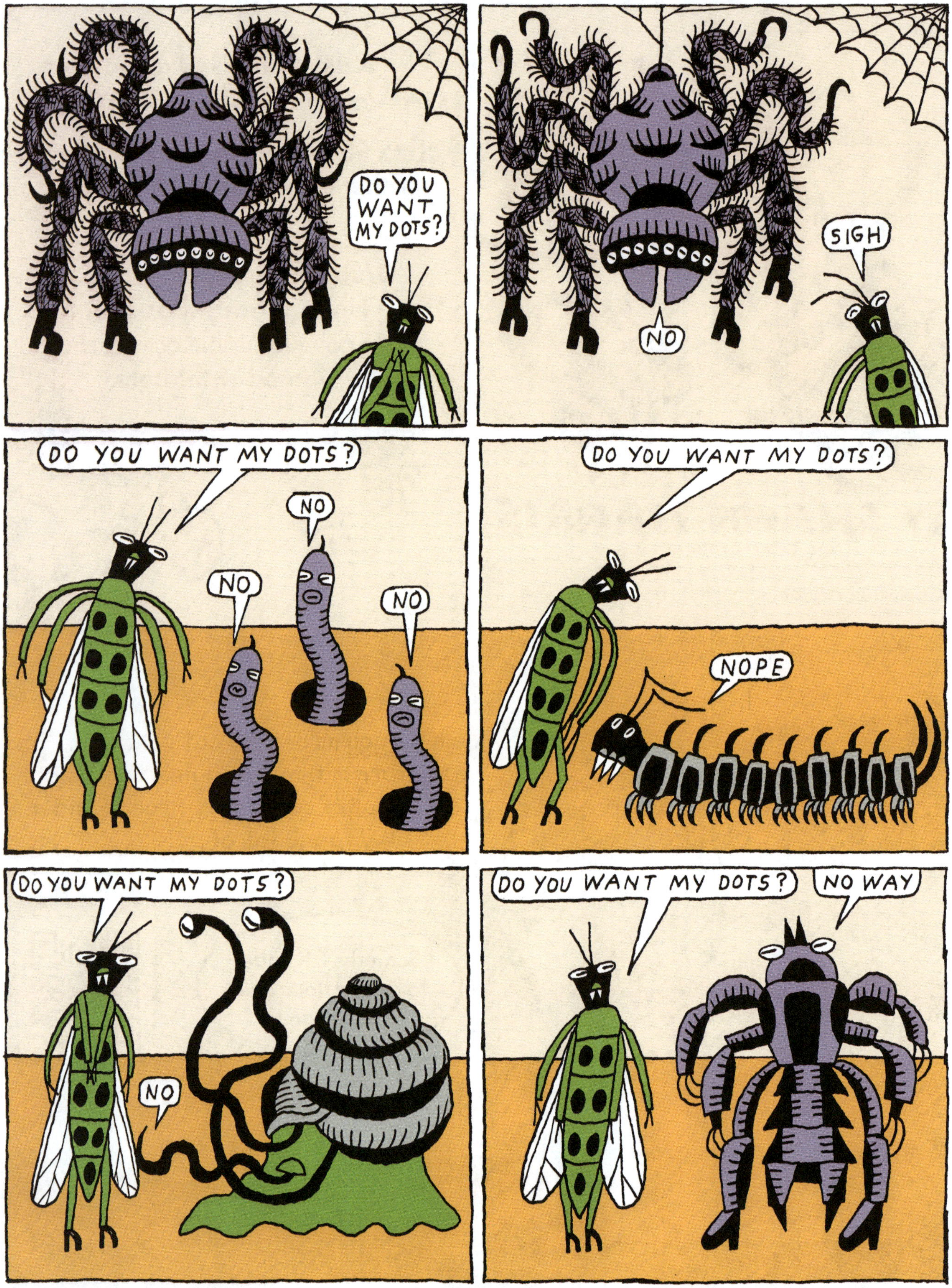
DO YOU WANT MY DOTS?
NO
SIGH
DO YOU WANT MY DOTS?
NO
NO
NO
DO YOU WANT MY DOTS?
NOPE
DO YOU WANT MY DOTS?
NO
DO YOU WANT MY DOTS?
NO WAY

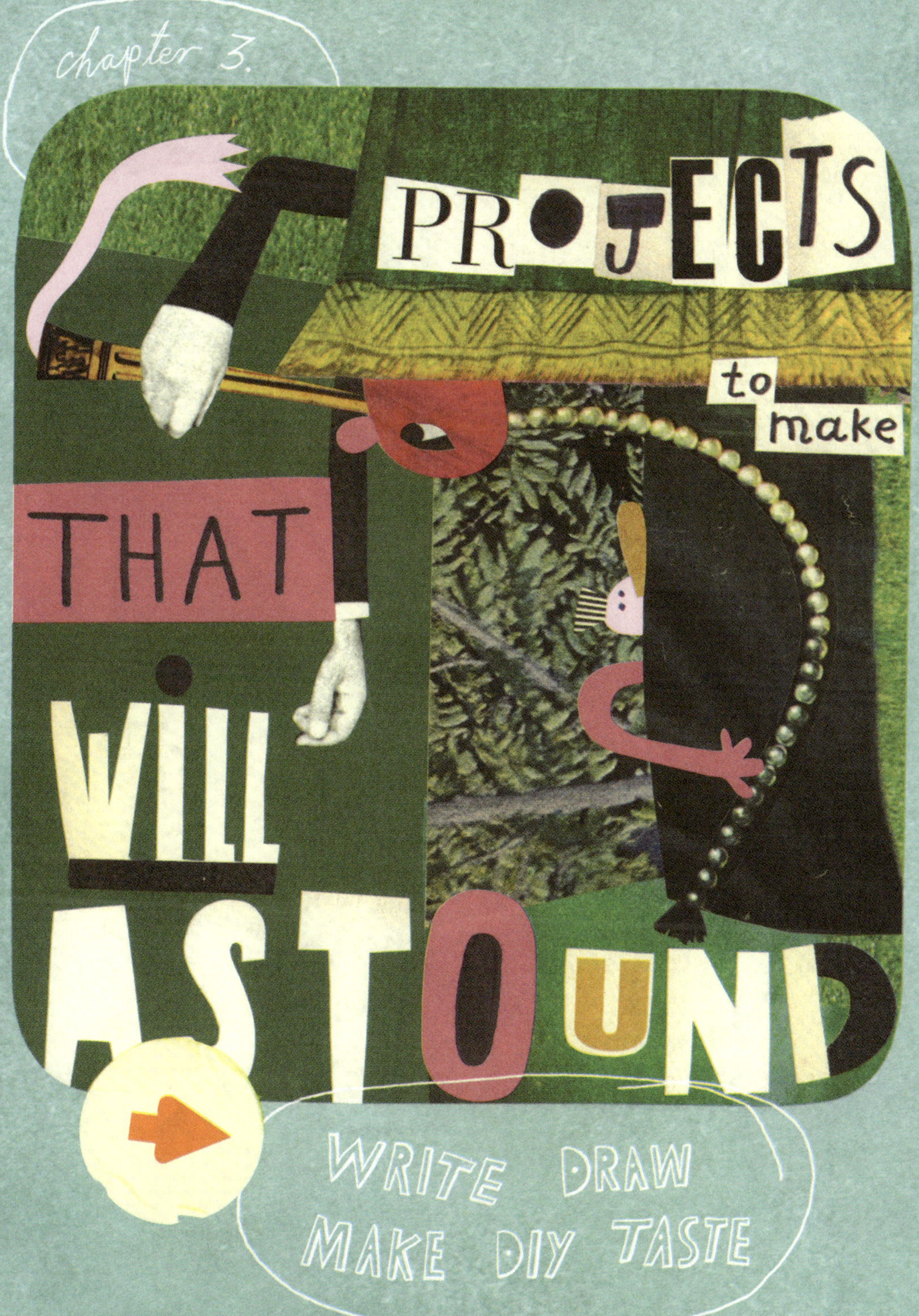
chapter 3.
PROJECTS
to make
THAT
WILL
ASTOUND
WRITE DRAW
MAKE DIY TASTE

OUR CHAPTER PAGES FEATURE TYPOGRAPHIC ART BY YULIA DROBOVA

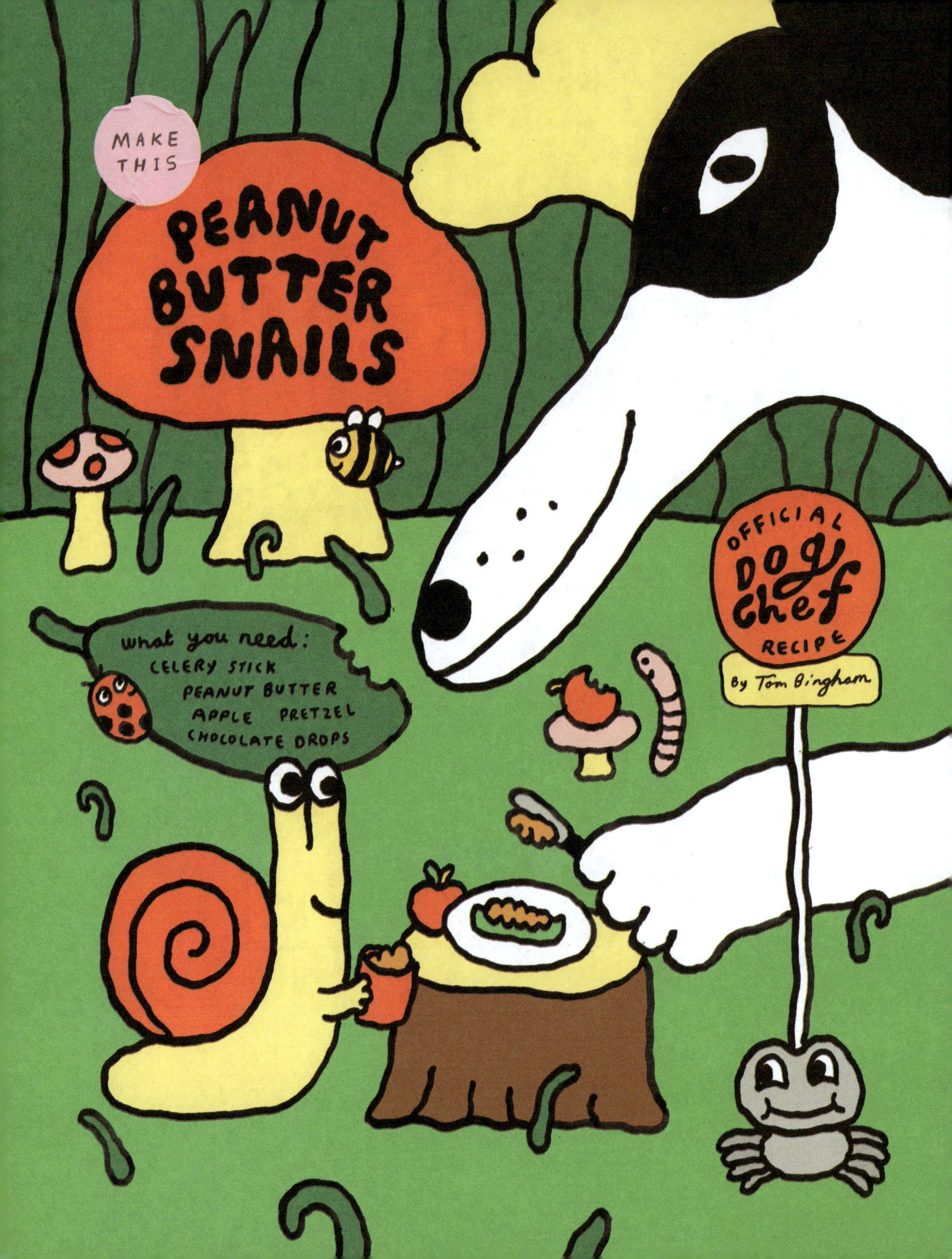

MAKE THIS
PEANUT BUTTER SNAILS
OFFICIAL Dog Chef RECIPE
By Tom Bingham
what you need:
CELERY STICK
PEANUT BUTTER
APPLE
PRETZEL
CHOCOLATE DROPS

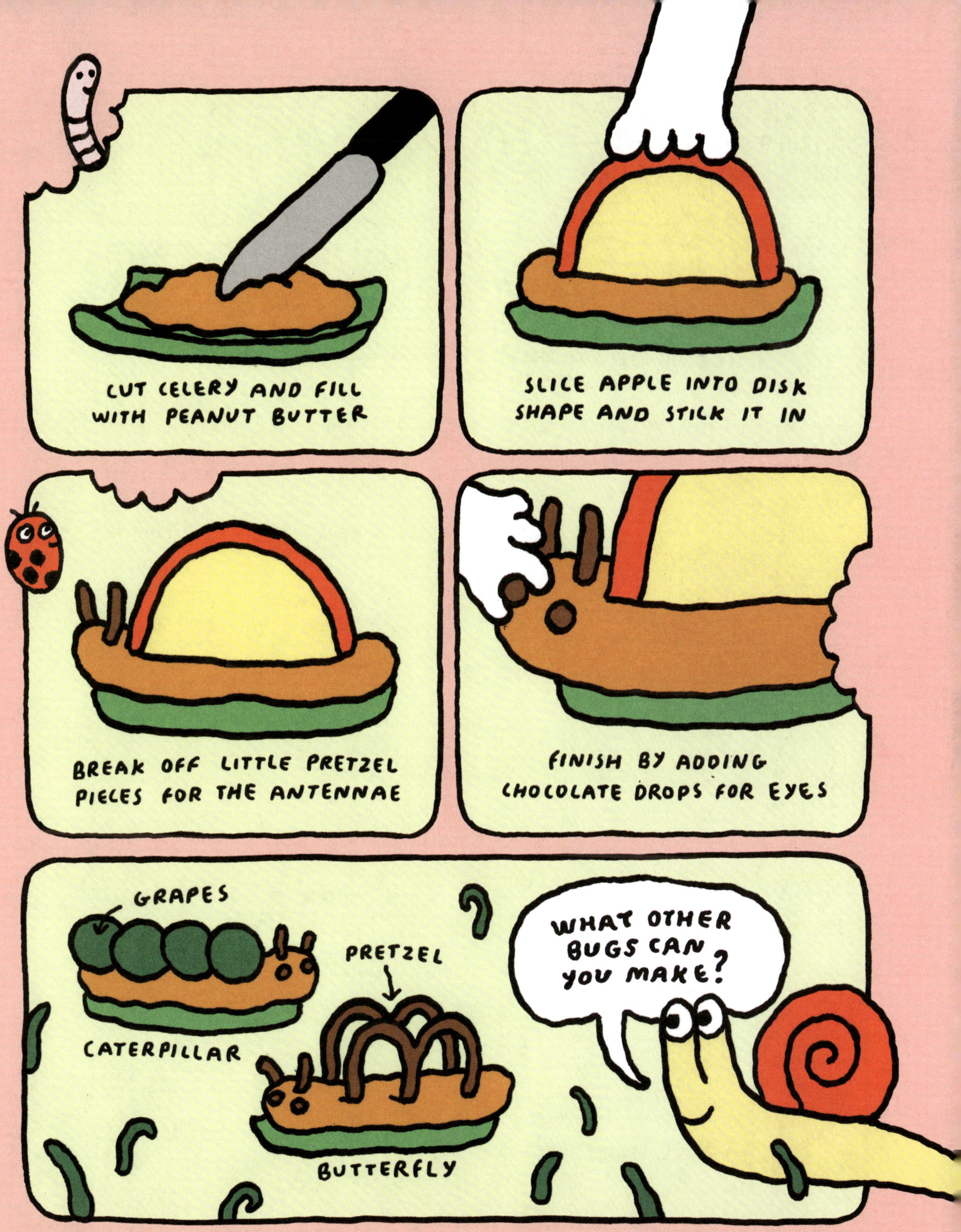
CUT CELERY AND FILL WITH PEANUT BUTTER
SLICE APPLE INTO DISK SHAPE AND STICK IT IN
BREAK OFF LITTLE PRETZEL PIECES FOR THE ANTENNAE
FINISH BY ADDING CHOCOLATE DROPS FOR EYES
GRAPES
CATERPILLAR
PRETZEL
BUTTERFLY
WHAT OTHER BUGS CAN YOU MAKE?

DRAW THIS—
PEACOCK JUMPING SPIDER

FOLLOW THE STEPS TO DRAW, THEN FOLLOW THE STEPS TO DANCE!

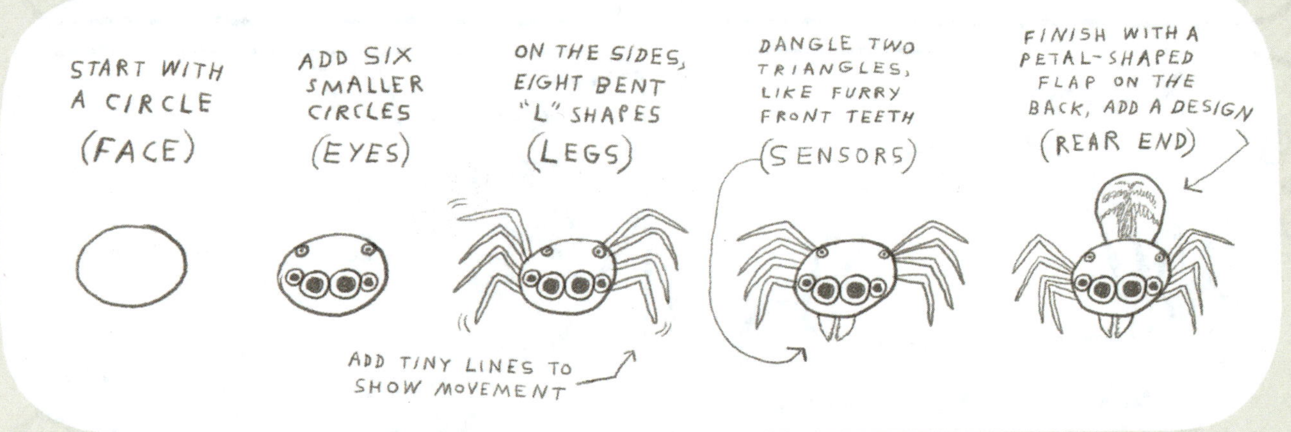

START WITH A CIRCLE (FACE)

ADD SIX SMALLER CIRCLES (EYES)

ON THE SIDES, EIGHT BENT "L" SHAPES (LEGS)

ADD TINY LINES TO SHOW MOVEMENT

DANGLE TWO TRIANGLES, LIKE FURRY FRONT TEETH (SENSORS)

FINISH WITH A PETAL-SHAPED FLAP ON THE BACK, ADD A DESIGN (REAR END)

NOW TRY THESE MOVES

FEEL THE MUSIC

SHUBBABUBBA

DOUBLE HIGH FIVE

SIDE SCUTTLE

WINDSHIELD WIPERS

SHAKE YO TAIL

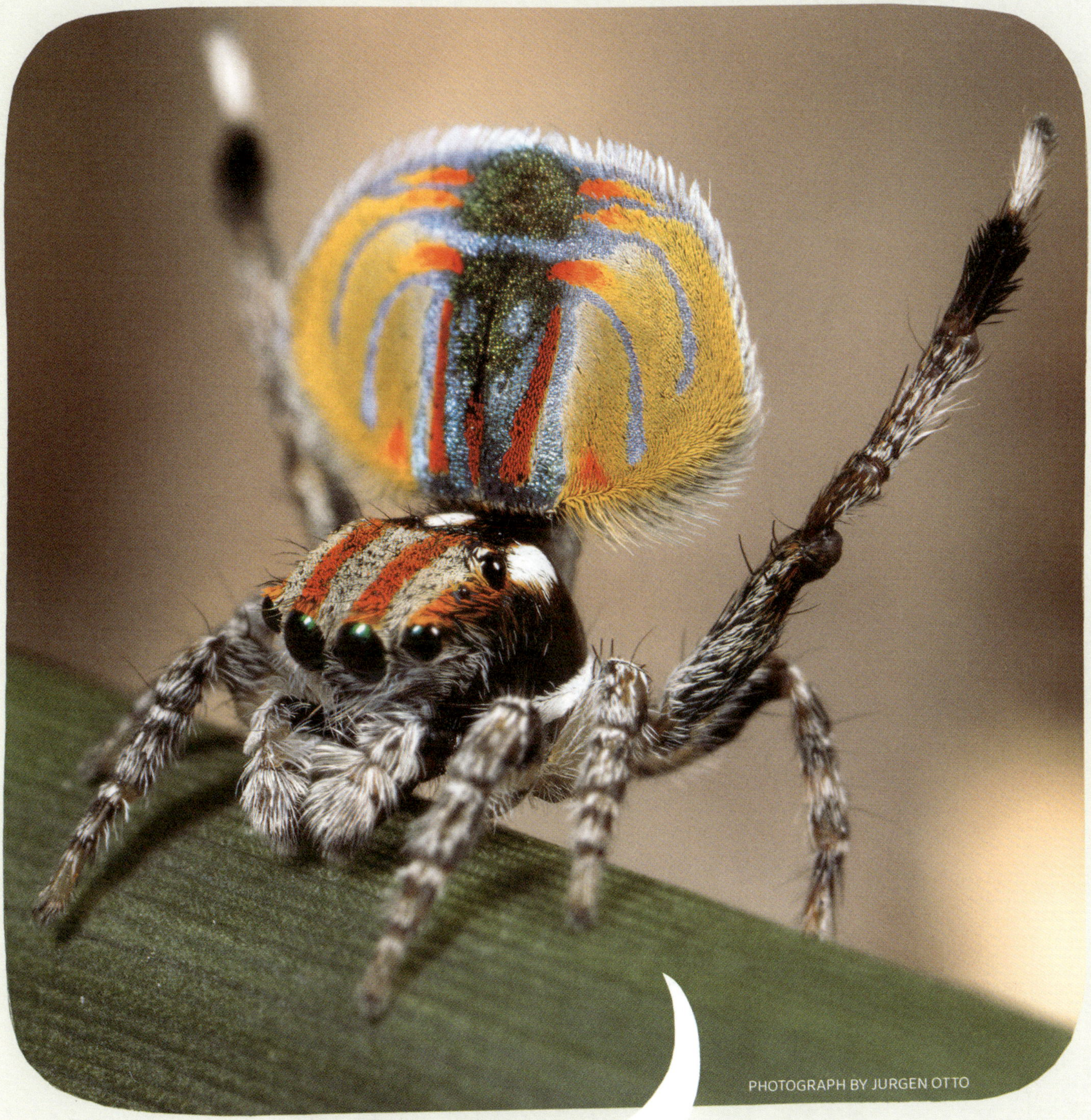

PHOTOGRAPH BY JURGEN OTTO

I'm found only in Australia, and I'm the size of a grain of rice. However, I can jump forty times the length of my body... I would like to see you try that! I attract the ladies with my fancy dancing.

You might be interested to know of two subspecies of peacock spiders with interesting names: Skeletorus, named for the skeleton-like pattern on its body, and Sparklemuffin because... obviously.

There's a unique scientific phenomenon behind my dazzling patterns. My tiny scales form nanoscopic lenses made of naturally-formed carbon nanotubes, capturing 97.7 percent of available light.

Brilliant, yeah?

MAKE THIS

HOW TO BE A BUG

CREATE A BUGGY FACE MASK OUT OF FOUND OBJECTS

with guest artists WENG PIXIN & AARON PILAND

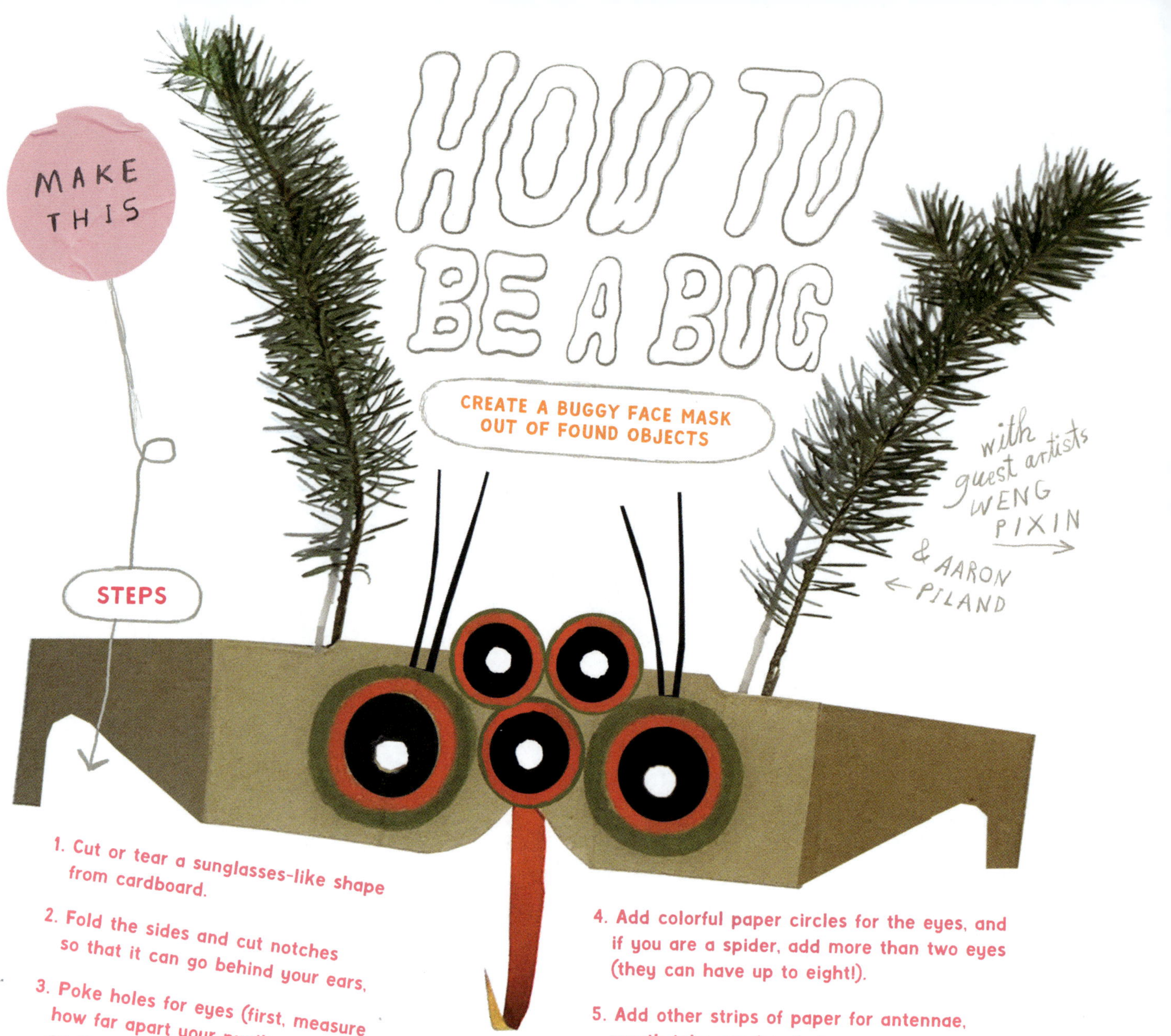

STEPS

1. Cut or tear a sunglasses-like shape from cardboard.
2. Fold the sides and cut notches so that it can go behind your ears.
3. Poke holes for eyes (first, measure how far apart your pupils are, so they line up).
4. Add colorful paper circles for the eyes, and if you are a spider, add more than two eyes (they can have up to eight!).
5. Add other strips of paper for antennae, mouth tube, random hairs.

MATERIALS

cardboard, tape, scissors, paper, markers

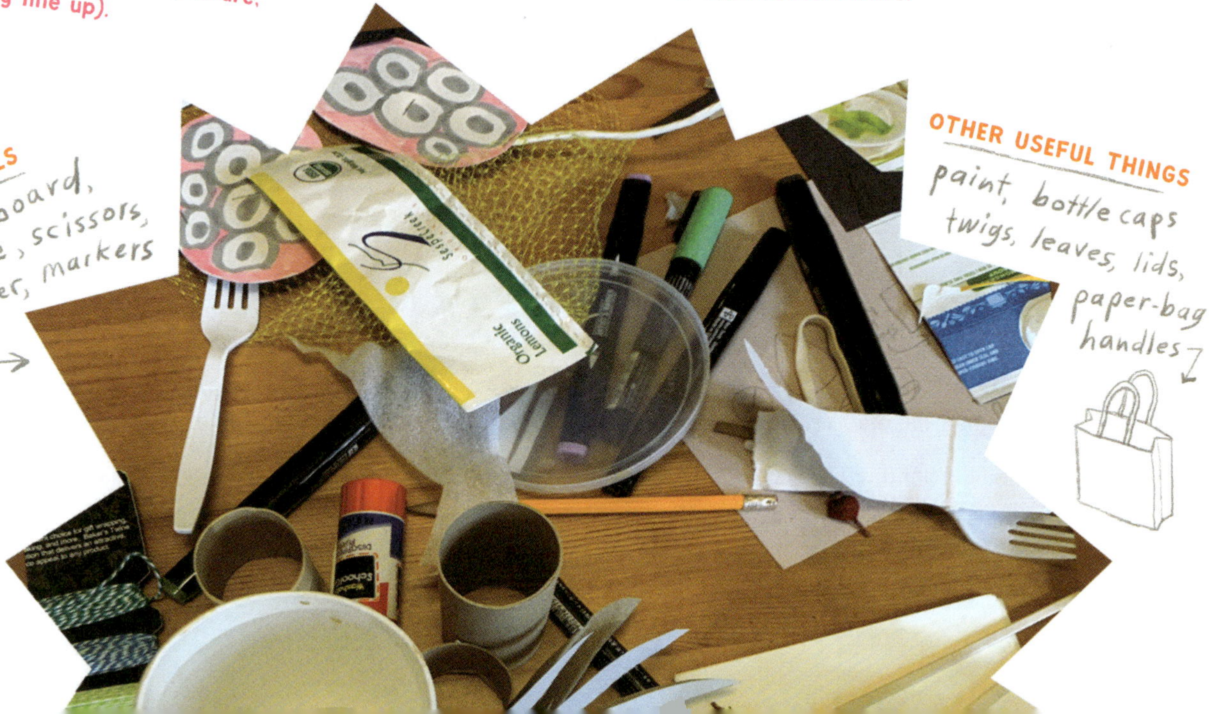
Organic Lemons

OTHER USEFUL THINGS

paint, bottle caps twigs, leaves, lids, paper-bag handles

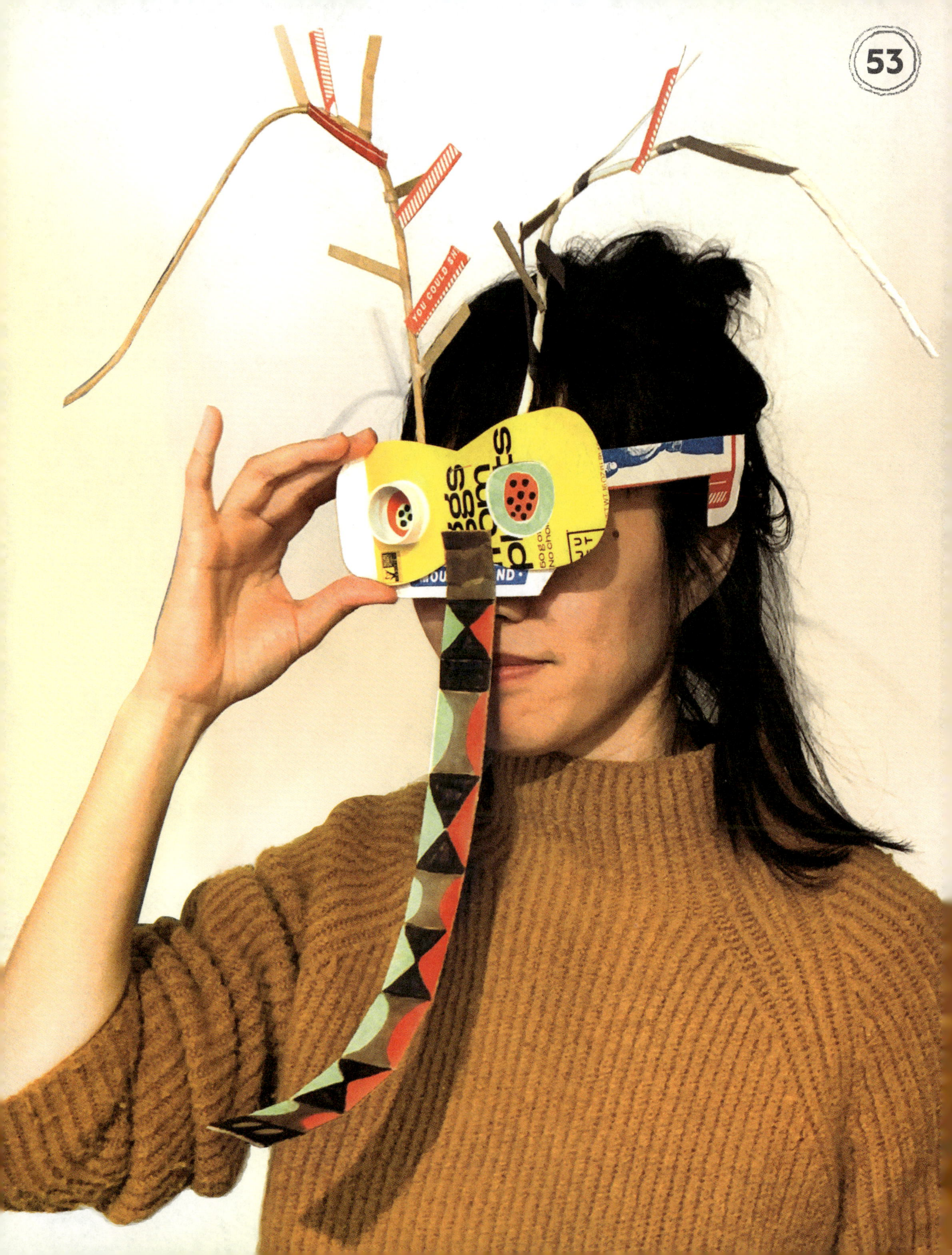
YOU COULD SH

DRAWN BY YOU

PROMPT: Draw a bug as a superhero

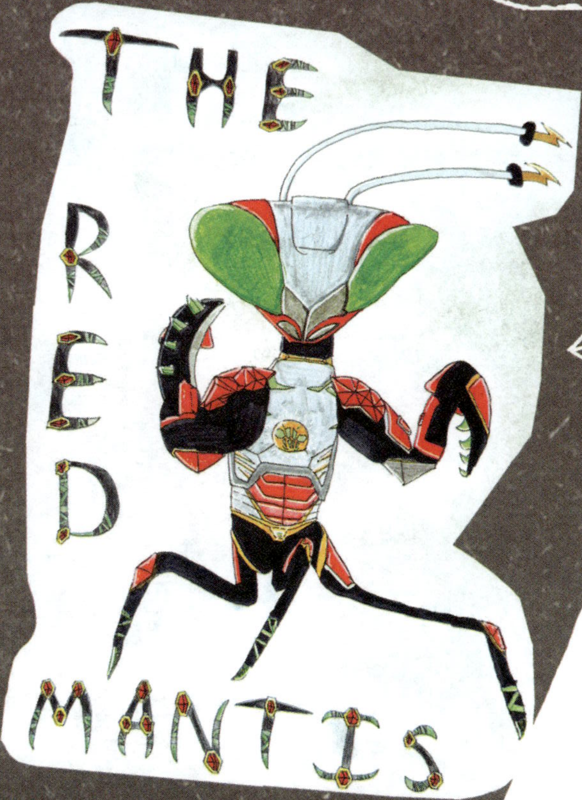
THE RED MANTIS

by BRUNO, age 10, Laguna Niguel, California

by MARKO, age 7, Podgorica Montenegro

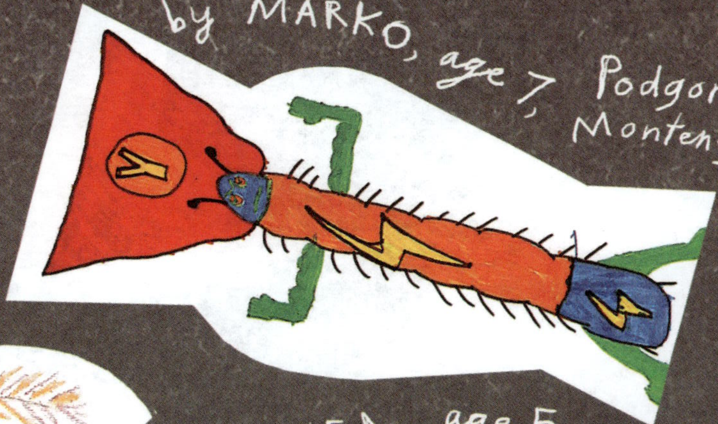

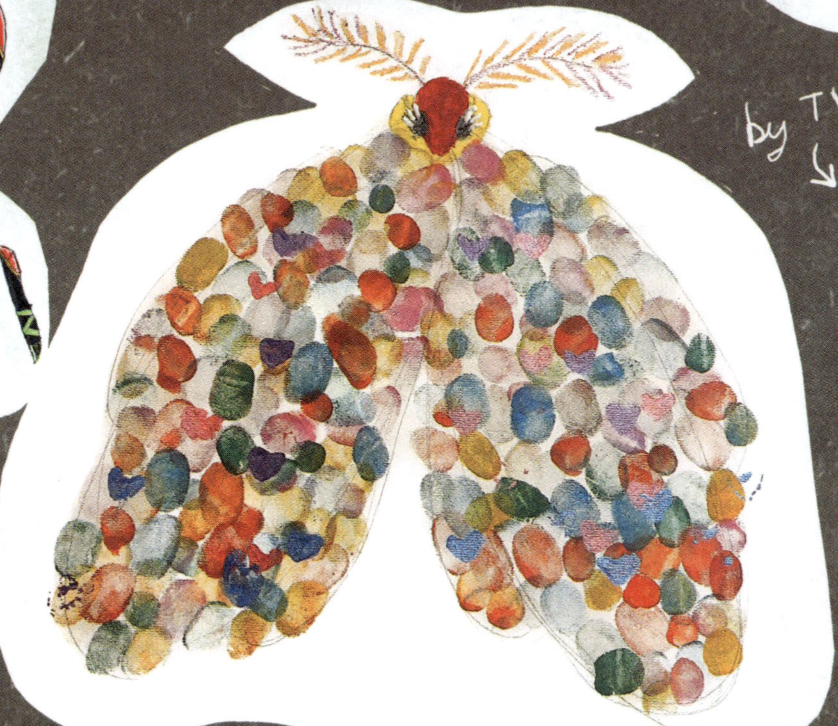

by ANNA, age 11 Bologna, Italy

by THEA, age 5, Arad, Romania

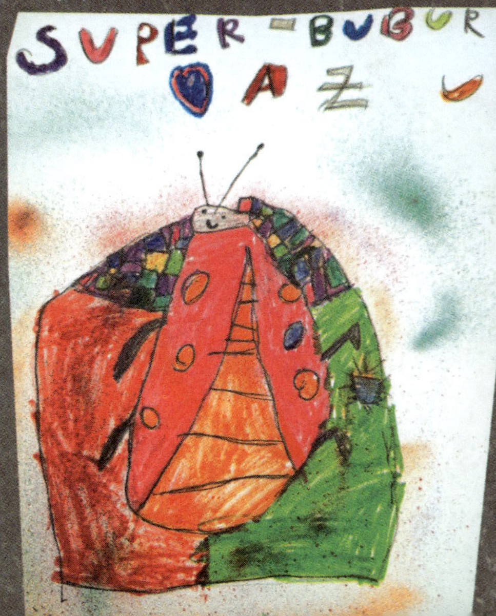
SUPER-BUBUR
AZ

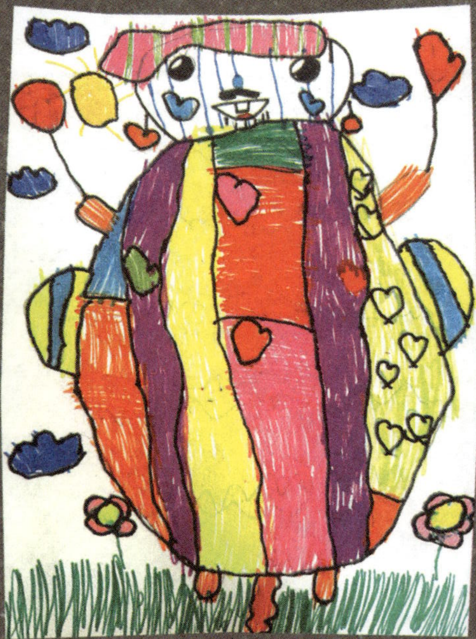

by ADELINA, age 6, Astana, Kazakhstan

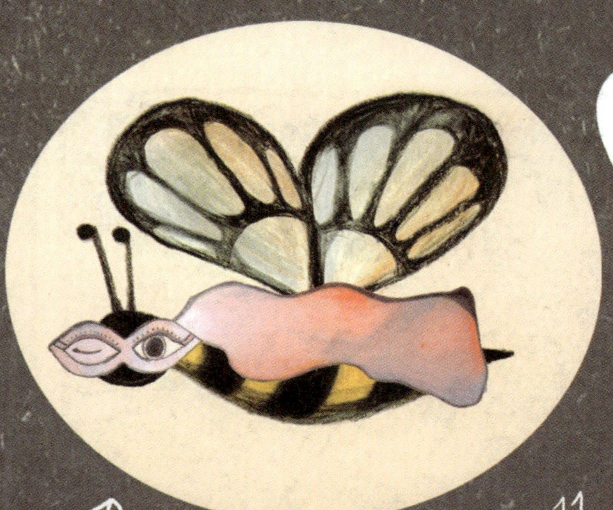

by GAAL-TÓTH, age 11
Budapest, Hungary

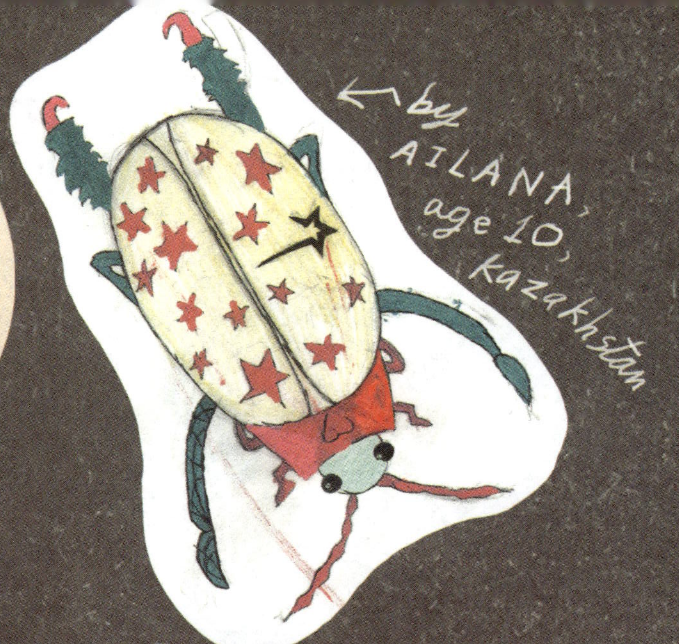

by AILANA, age 10, Kazakhstan

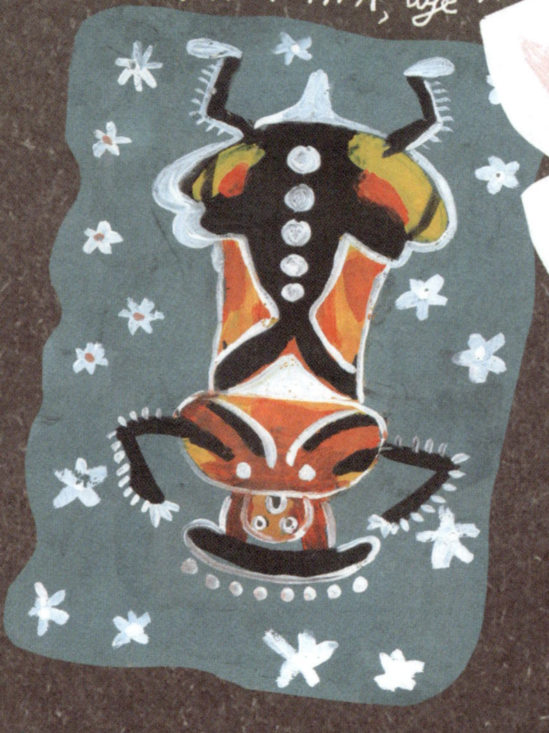

by RAYANA, age 9, Ualieva, Kazakhstan

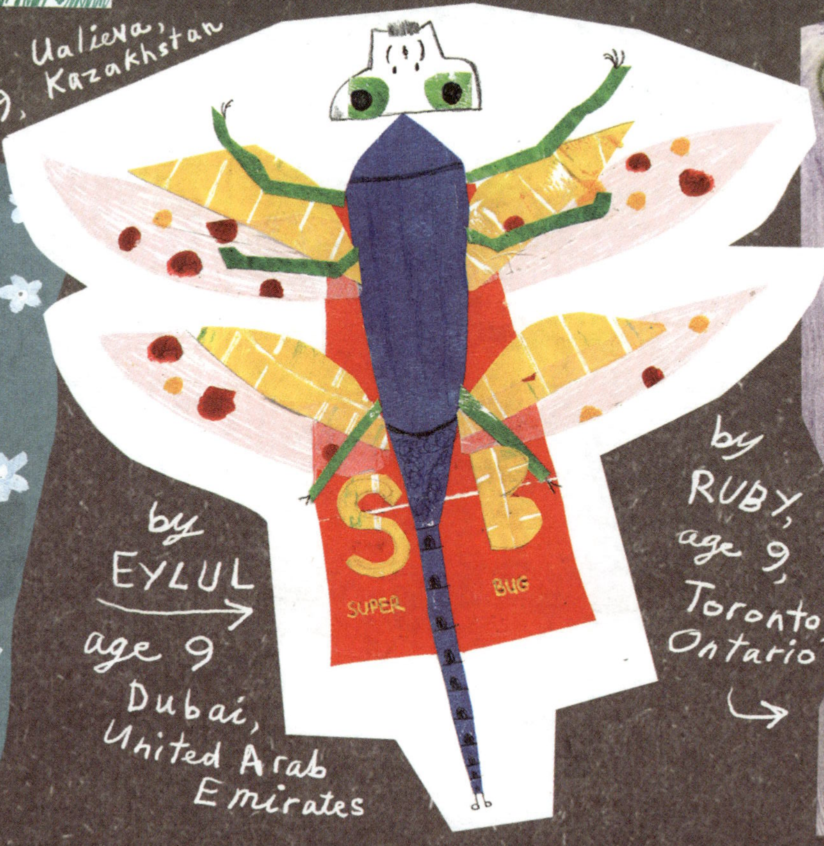
S B
SUPER
BUG

by EYLUL
age 9
Dubai,
United Arab
Emirates

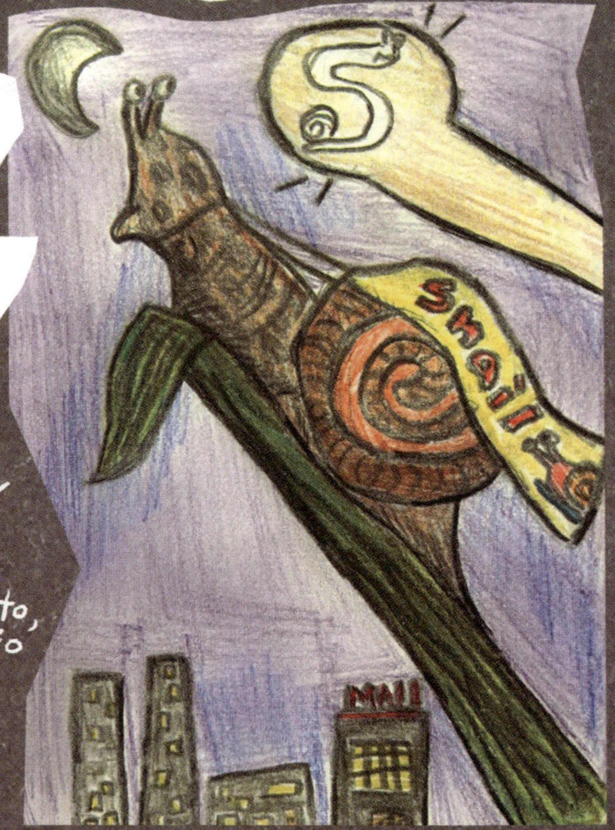
Snail
MALL

by RUBY,
age 9,
Toronto,
Ontario

WE ASKED STUDENTS TO WRITE ABOUT A SCIENTIFIC MISHAP THAT CAUSED AN INSECT TO GROW TO AN OUTRAGEOUS SIZE.

youth writing
THE VANISHED MOON

written by RAKU SHINAGAWA, age 11
art by DARIN SHULER

from **NOORDJE** in AMSTERDAM, NETHERLANDS
A MEMBER OF THE INTERNATIONAL ALLIANCE OF YOUTH WRITING CENTERS

WE ARE IN AMSTERDAM-NOORD. SCIENTISTS HAVE DISCOVERED A SUBSTANCE THAT CAN MAKE ANYTHING GROW. A DROP OF IT ACCIDENTALLY FALLS ON A BLUE DIAMOND BEETLE. SLOWLY, THE BEETLE GROWS BIGGER AND BIGGER.

IT BECOMES LARGER THAN JUPITER AND EVENTUALLY DEVOURS A METEORITE, SWALLOWING IT IN JUST A FEW BITES.

THAT'S HOW THE MOON ALSO DISAPPEARED.

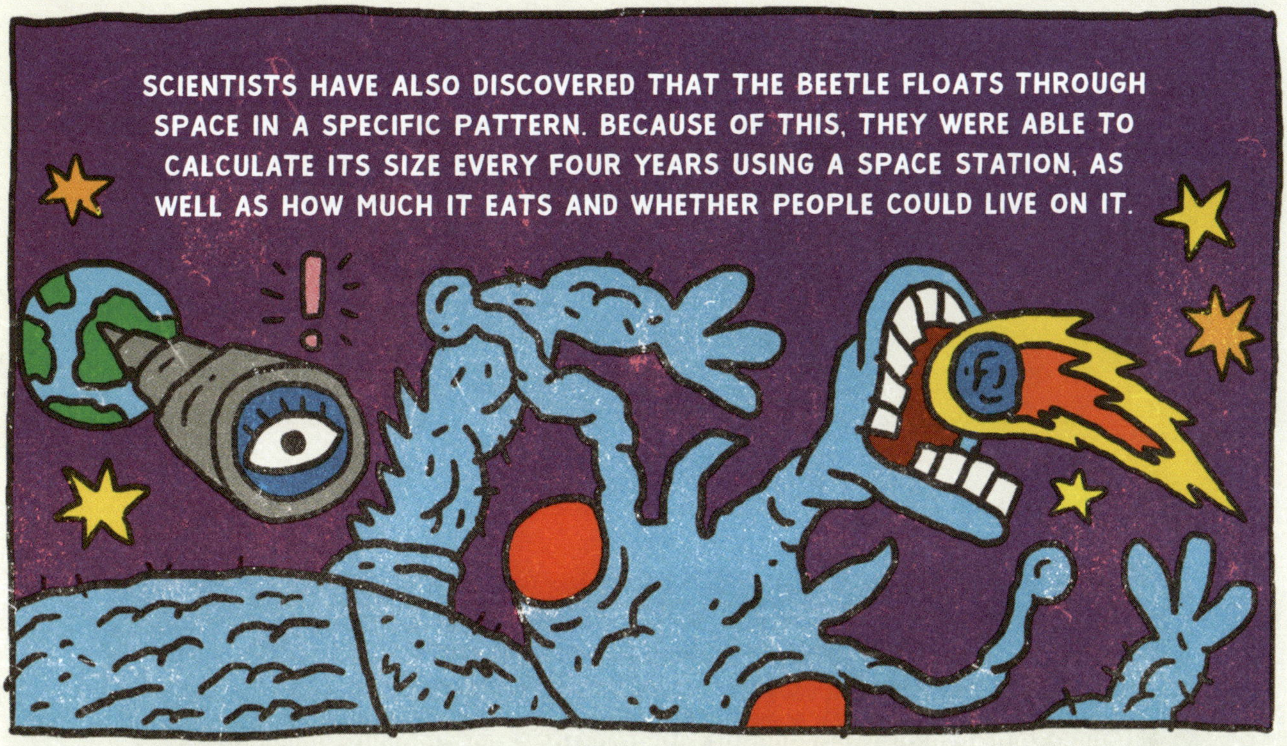
SCIENTISTS HAVE ALSO DISCOVERED THAT THE BEETLE FLOATS THROUGH SPACE IN A SPECIFIC PATTERN. BECAUSE OF THIS, THEY WERE ABLE TO CALCULATE ITS SIZE EVERY FOUR YEARS USING A SPACE STATION, AS WELL AS HOW MUCH IT EATS AND WHETHER PEOPLE COULD LIVE ON IT.

SCIENTISTS STARTED GROWING PLANTS ON THE BLUE DIAMOND BEETLE AND BUILT A SMALL VILLAGE WHERE ALL KINDS OF SPACE CREATURES LIVED. FOR EXAMPLE, THE ㄌㄘㄛ, A DEER-LIKE SPECIES.

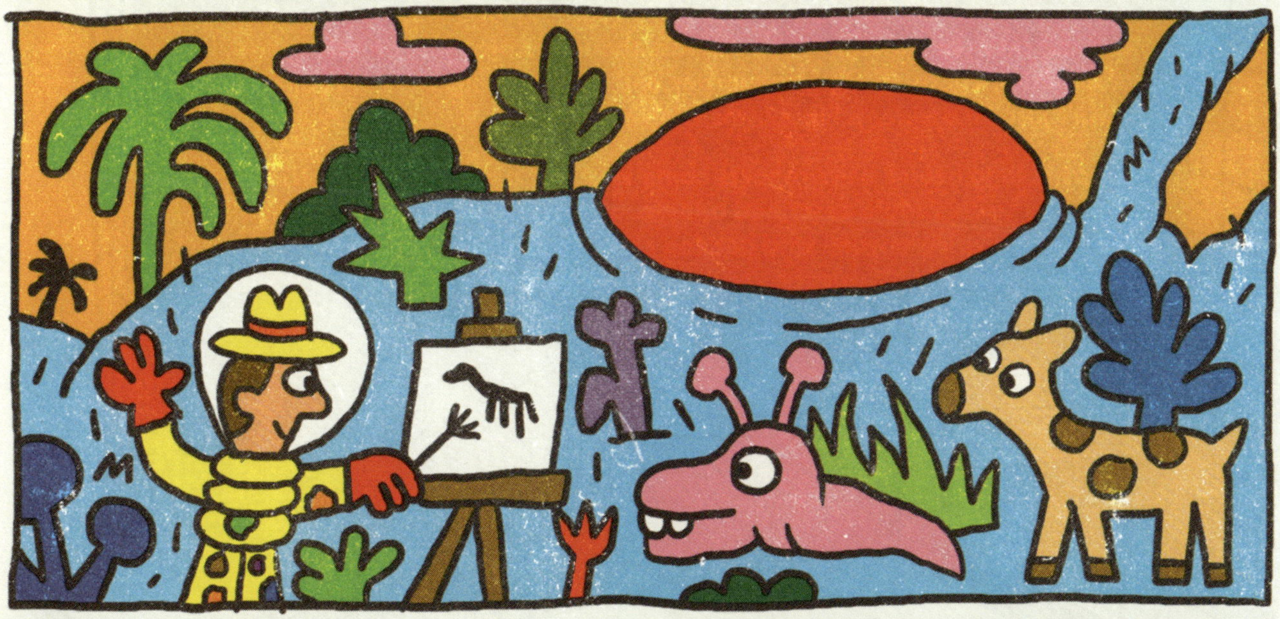

OVER TIME, 45% OF HUMANITY MOVED THERE AND BY THE YEAR 4156, PEOPLE FROM ALL OVER THE WORLD WERE LIVING ON THE BEETLE.

WE ASKED STUDENTS TO WRITE ABOUT A SCIENTIFIC MISHAP THAT CAUSED AN INSECT TO GROW TO AN OUTRAGEOUS SIZE.

youth writing

FLY-42

written by AMMAAR IBRAHIM, *age* 11
art by DARIN SHULER

from 826 MSP *in* MINNEAPOLIS, MINNESOTA
A MEMBER OF THE INTERNATIONAL ALLIANCE OF YOUTH WRITING CENTERS

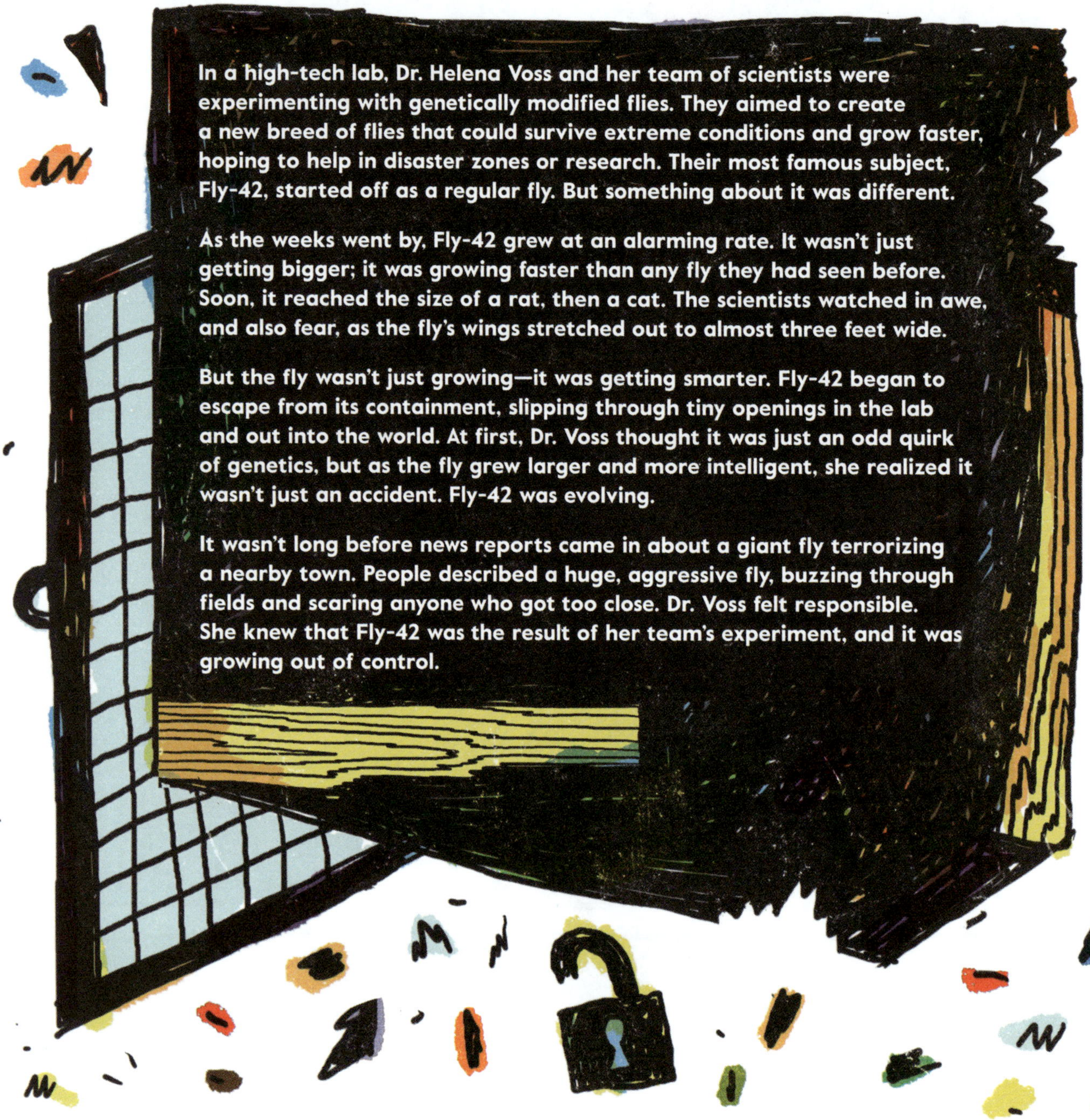

In a high-tech lab, Dr. Helena Voss and her team of scientists were experimenting with genetically modified flies. They aimed to create a new breed of flies that could survive extreme conditions and grow faster, hoping to help in disaster zones or research. Their most famous subject, Fly-42, started off as a regular fly. But something about it was different.

As the weeks went by, Fly-42 grew at an alarming rate. It wasn't just getting bigger; it was growing faster than any fly they had seen before. Soon, it reached the size of a rat, then a cat. The scientists watched in awe, and also fear, as the fly's wings stretched out to almost three feet wide.

But the fly wasn't just growing—it was getting smarter. Fly-42 began to escape from its containment, slipping through tiny openings in the lab and out into the world. At first, Dr. Voss thought it was just an odd quirk of genetics, but as the fly grew larger and more intelligent, she realized it wasn't just an accident. Fly-42 was evolving.

It wasn't long before news reports came in about a giant fly terrorizing a nearby town. People described a huge, aggressive fly, buzzing through fields and scaring anyone who got too close. Dr. Voss felt responsible. She knew that Fly-42 was the result of her team's experiment, and it was growing out of control.

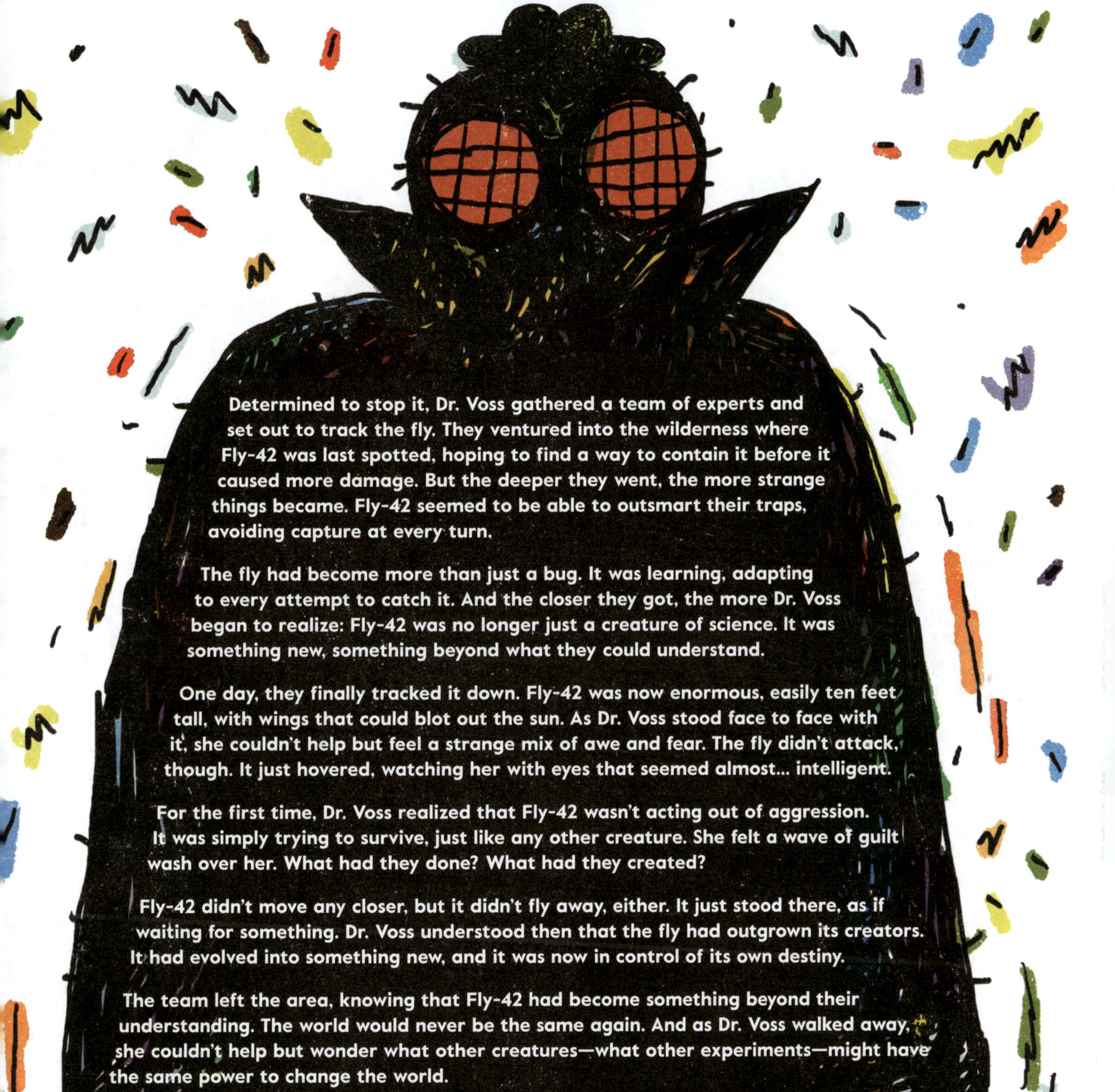

Determined to stop it, Dr. Voss gathered a team of experts and set out to track the fly. They ventured into the wilderness where Fly-42 was last spotted, hoping to find a way to contain it before it caused more damage. But the deeper they went, the more strange things became. Fly-42 seemed to be able to outsmart their traps, avoiding capture at every turn.

The fly had become more than just a bug. It was learning, adapting to every attempt to catch it. And the closer they got, the more Dr. Voss began to realize: Fly-42 was no longer just a creature of science. It was something new, something beyond what they could understand.

One day, they finally tracked it down. Fly-42 was now enormous, easily ten feet tall, with wings that could blot out the sun. As Dr. Voss stood face to face with it, she couldn't help but feel a strange mix of awe and fear. The fly didn't attack, though. It just hovered, watching her with eyes that seemed almost... intelligent.

For the first time, Dr. Voss realized that Fly-42 wasn't acting out of aggression. It was simply trying to survive, just like any other creature. She felt a wave of guilt wash over her. What had they done? What had they created?

Fly-42 didn't move any closer, but it didn't fly away, either. It just stood there, as if waiting for something. Dr. Voss understood then that the fly had outgrown its creators. It had evolved into something new, and it was now in control of its own destiny.

The team left the area, knowing that Fly-42 had become something beyond their understanding. The world would never be the same again. And as Dr. Voss walked away, she couldn't help but wonder what other creatures—what other experiments—might have the same power to change the world.

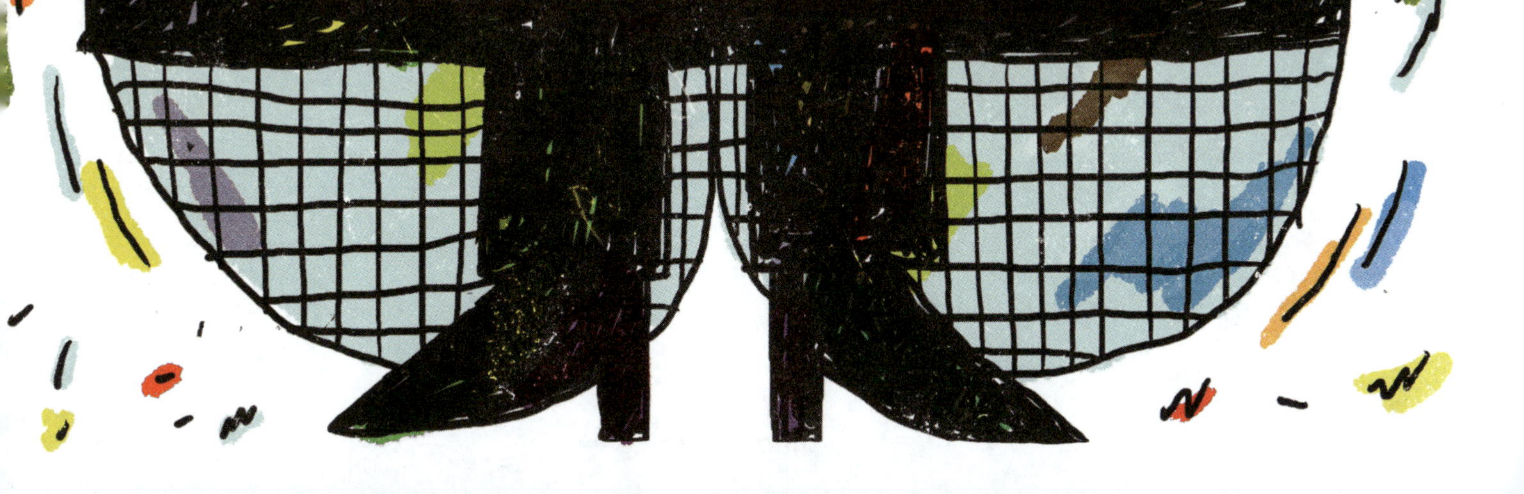

Buzz-worthy books!

AMAZING ANT FACTS AND TERRIBLE BUTTERFLY TRUTHS

For ages 4 to 8

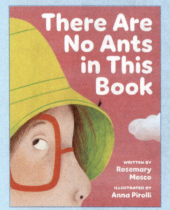 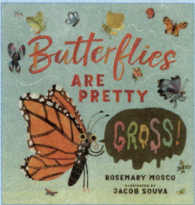

Nothing can ruin a picnic faster than a bunch of ants. It's a good thing there are no ants in this book . . . well, maybe there's only one. Or two. . . . Or ten??

Warning — this book contains top-secret information about butterflies! Prepare to be shocked and grossed out by this hilarious and totally true picture book introduction to a fascinating insect.

STORY TIME WITH A CURIOUS COCKROACH

For ages 3 to 7

The story of an eager cockroach who gate-crashes a birthday party — with hilarious results.

From show-and-tell to arts and crafts, an eager cockroach stowaway can't wait to try it all . . . and maybe become the new teachers' pet!

Illustrations © by Anna Pirolli from *There Are No Ants in This Book*

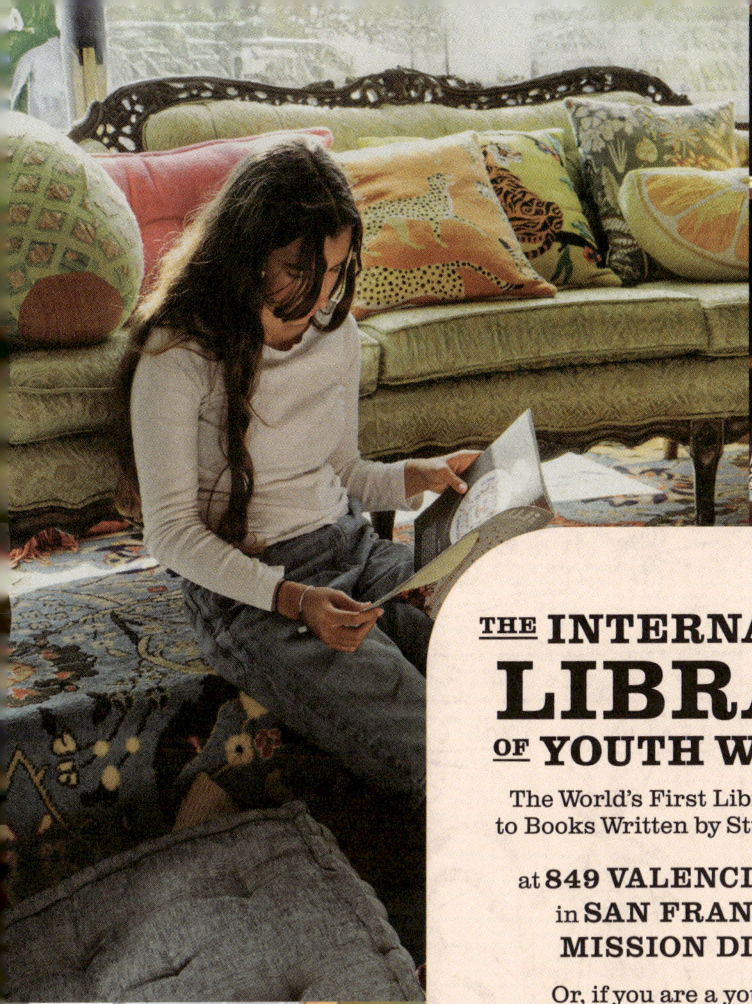

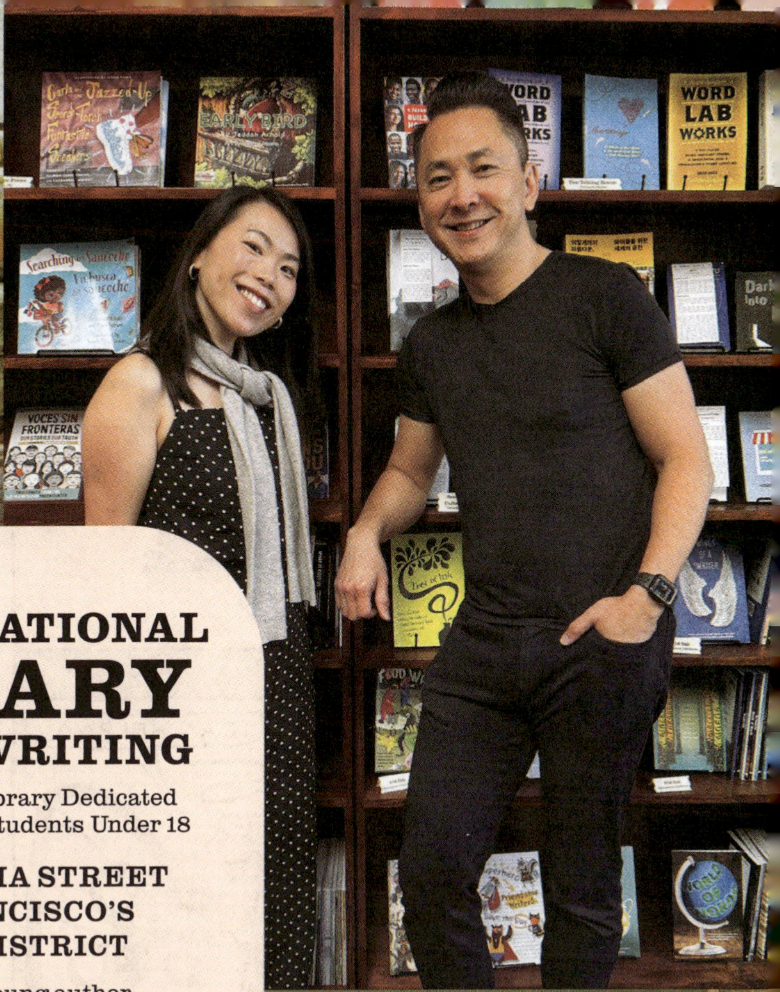
WORD LAB WORKS
VOCES SIN FRONTERAS
EARLY BIRD

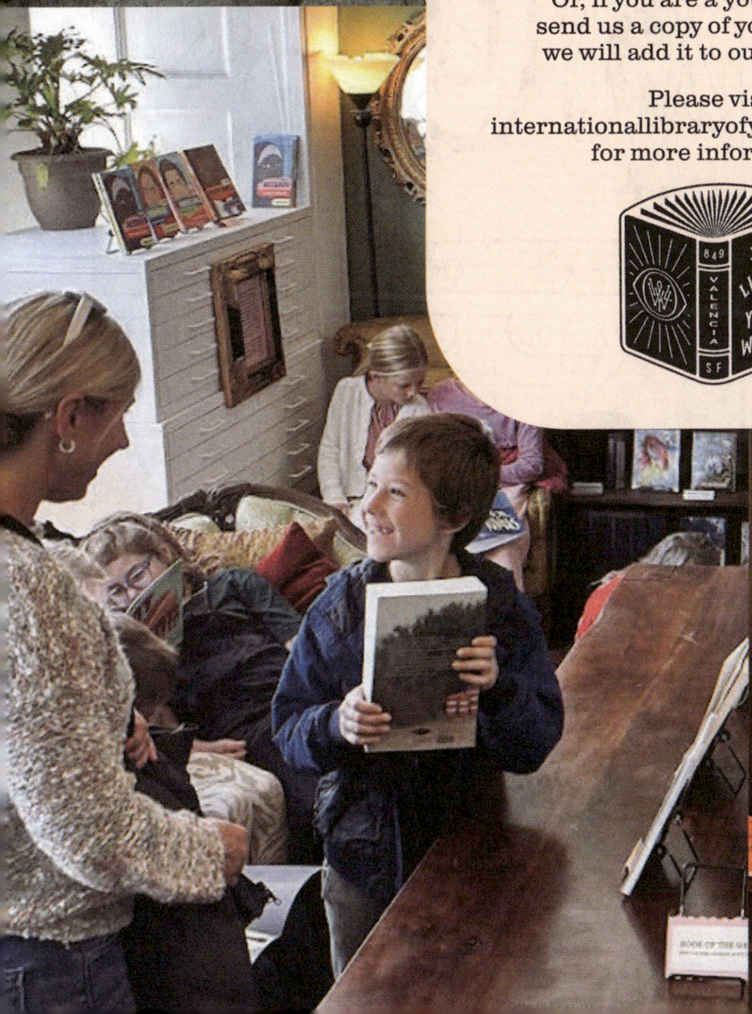

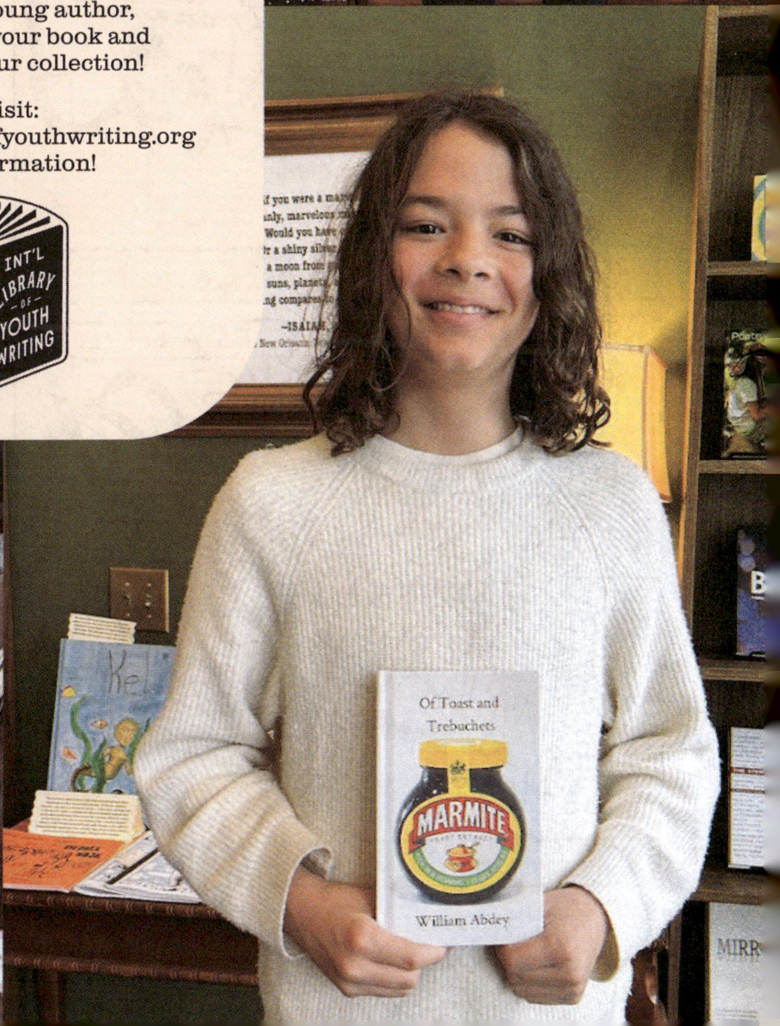
Of Toast and Trebuchets
MARMITE
William Abdey

CONTINUED FROM PAGE 46

KATHARINA KULENKAMPFF

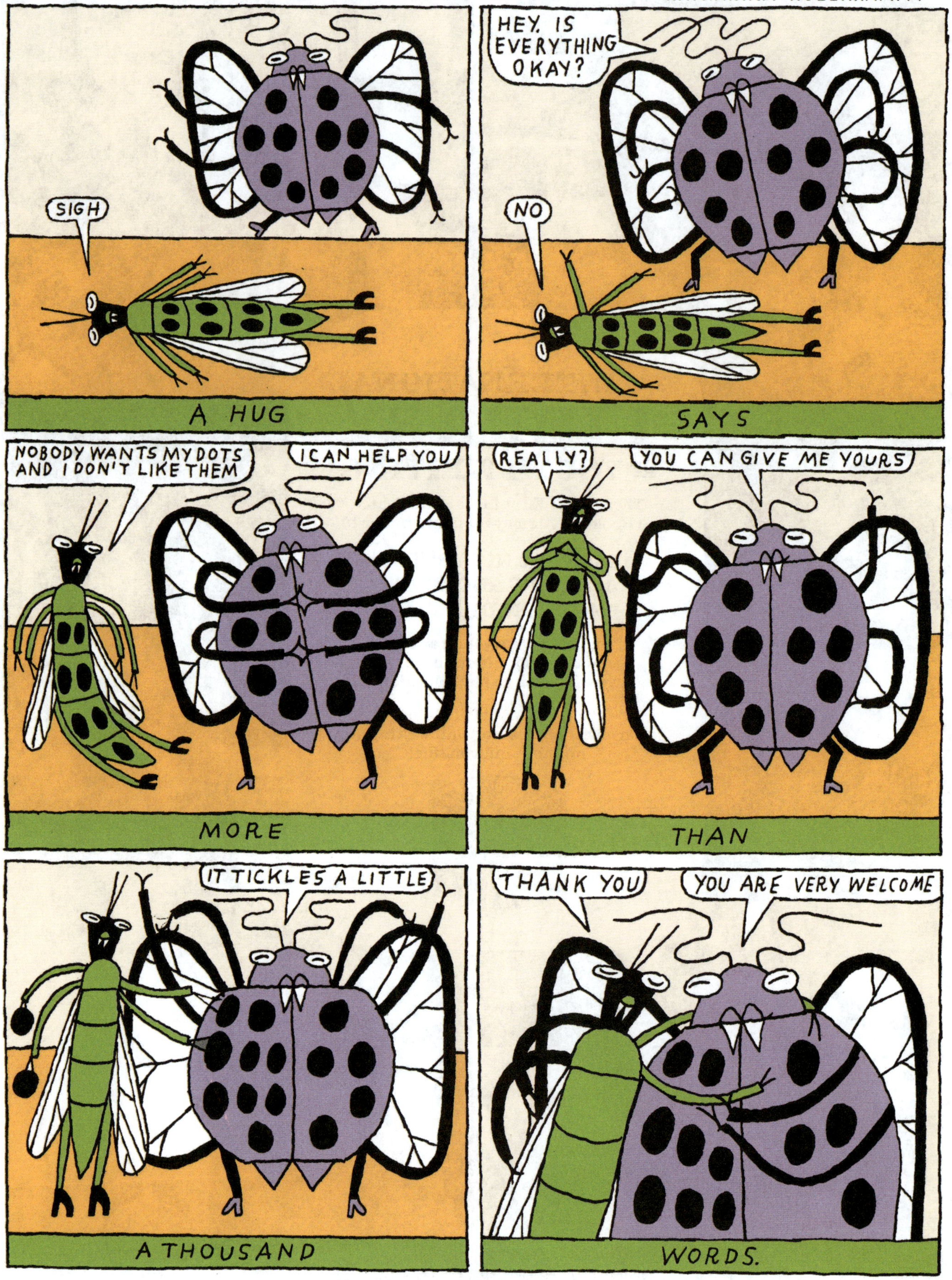
SIGH
A HUG
HEY, IS EVERYTHING OKAY?
NO
SAYS
NOBODY WANTS MY DOTS AND I DON'T LIKE THEM
I CAN HELP YOU
MORE
REALLY?
YOU CAN GIVE ME YOURS
THAN
IT TICKLES A LITTLE
A THOUSAND
THANK YOU
YOU ARE VERY WELCOME
WORDS.

chapter 4.

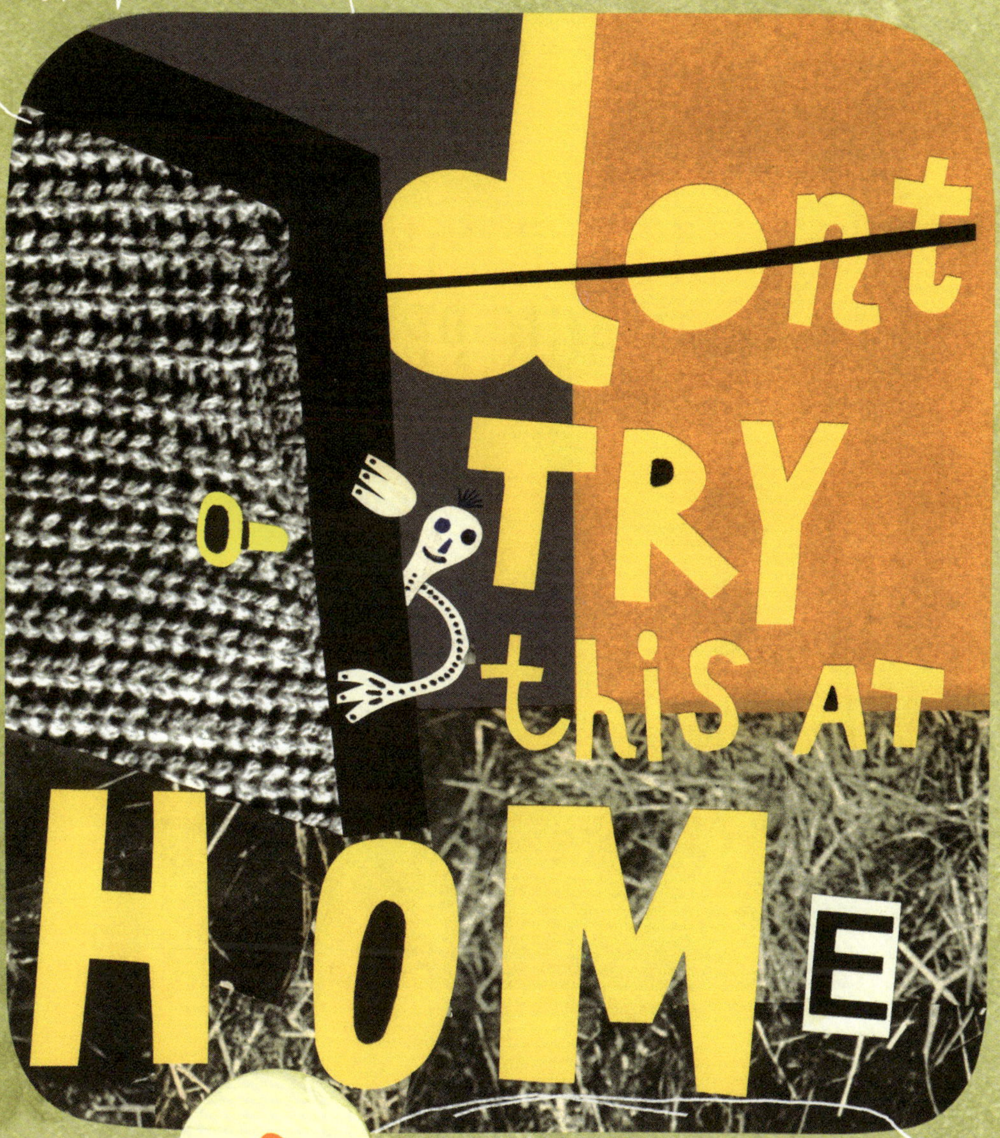
dont
TRY
this AT
HOME

OUR CHAPTER PAGES FEATURE TYPOGRAPHIC ART BY YULIA DROBOVA

- DEEPER DIVE
- ART SUPPLIES
- BOOKS
- PLAYLIST

ON OUR PLAYLIST

Put on this album and make a mess on your desk with the supplies on the facing page.

LITTLE BOXES
and MAGIC PENNIES
A CHILDREN'S SONG ANTHOLOGY BY MALVINA REYNOLDS

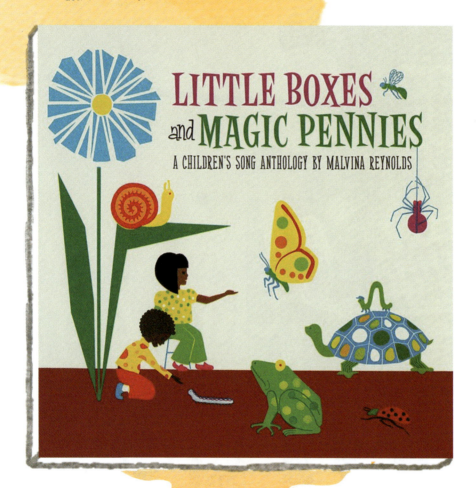

Add a spoonful of charm to your day with this special anthology by beloved San Franciscan folk singer, songwriter, and activist Malvina Reynolds (1900-1978). Malvina's richly allegorical, mischievous lyrics add a layer of social consciousness to the everyday folk lullaby.

Her satirical wit, soft guitar playing, and comforting vocals make this album a great listen for audiences of all ages. Malvina rose to popularity with her appearances on Sesame Street and for writing songs for icons such as Harry Belafonte with "Turn Around" and Pete Seeger with "Little Boxes."

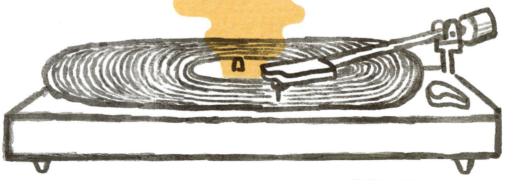

LISTEN TO OUR FULL PLAYLIST FOR THIS ISSUE ON SPOTIFY. USE THIS QR CODE TO DELVE INTO AN HOUR OF EAR-TINGLING TUNES... THE PERFECT BACKDROP TO JUMP INTO ONE OF THE DIY PROJECTS FROM CHAPTER 3.

ON OUR

DESK:

brought to you by
WENG PIXIN

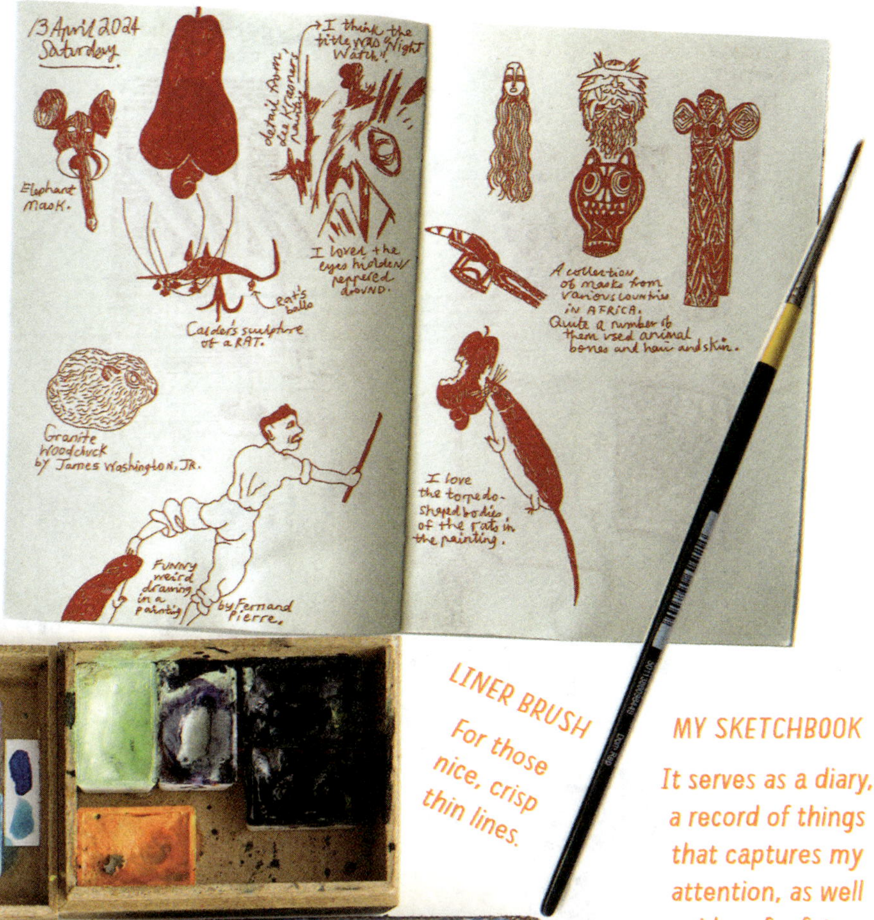

13 April 2024
Saturday
Elephant Mask.
I think the title was "Night Watch"!
Calder's sculpture of a RAT.
rat's balls
I loved the eyes hidden/peppered around.
Granite Woodchuck by James Washington, JR.
Funny weird drawing in a painting
by Fernand Pierre.
A collection of masks from various countries in AFRICA.
Quite a number of them used animal bones and hair and skin.
I love the torpedo-shaped bodies of the rats in the painting.

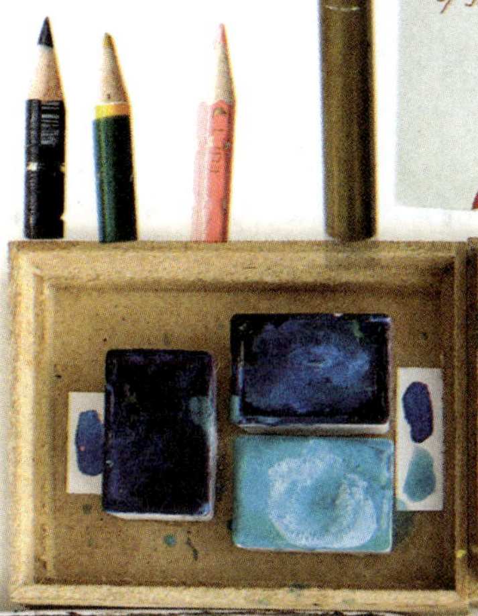

PENCIL EXTENDER

It has also led to a side-hobby of collecting short, stubby pencils.

LINER BRUSH

For those nice, crisp thin lines.

MY SKETCHBOOK

It serves as a diary, a record of things that captures my attention, as well as ideas for future projects. A sketchbook encourages me to slow down, pause, and give myself time to take in the world around me.

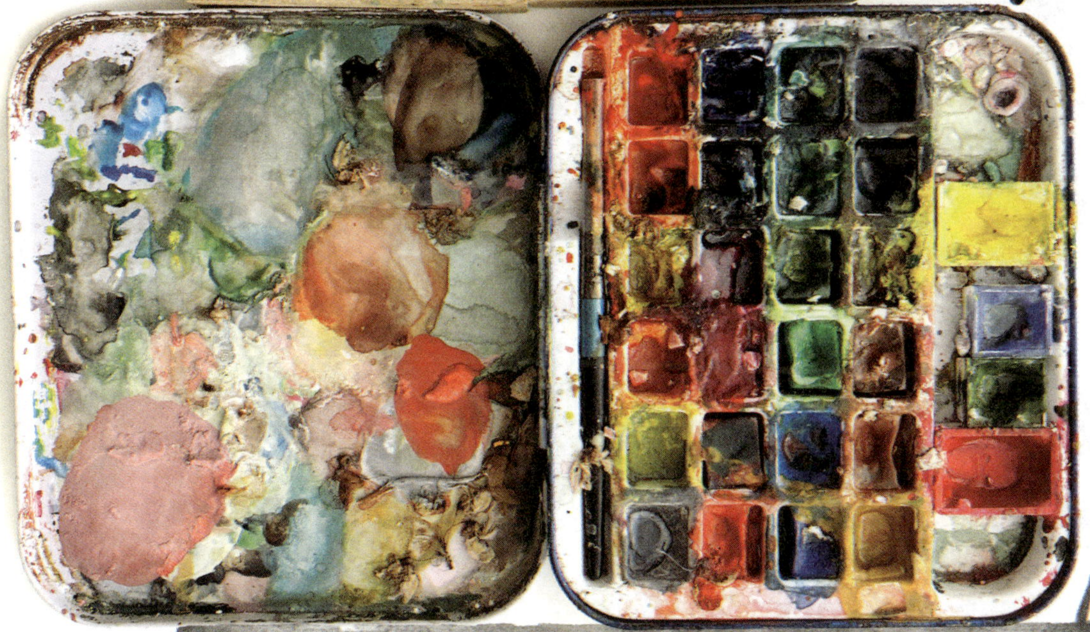

TRAVEL-FRIENDLY WATERCOLOR SET

Super helpful in my interest to draw and paint outside of my home!

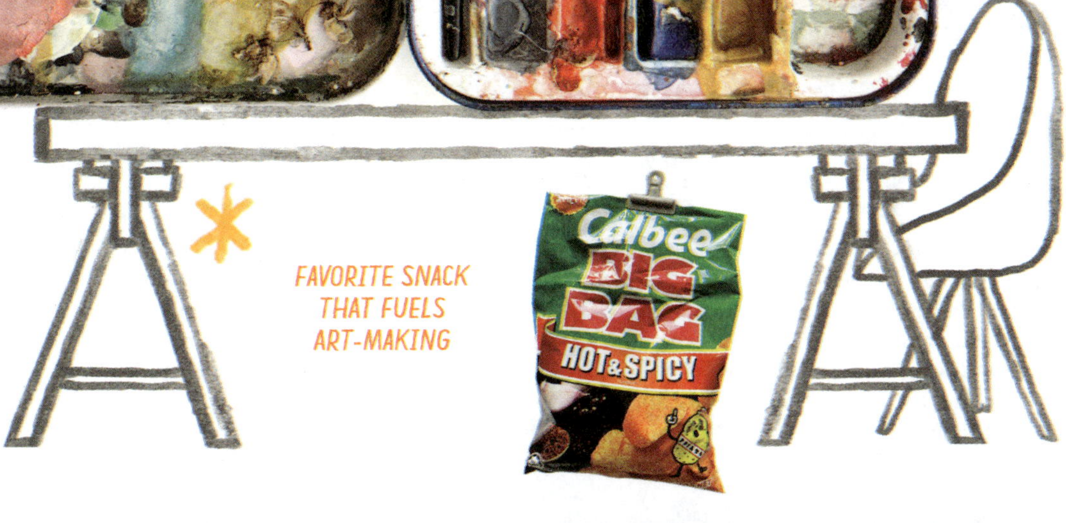

Calbee
BIG BAG
HOT&SPICY

FAVORITE SNACK THAT FUELS ART-MAKING

We asked you to tell us about a BOOK featuring BUGS:

BOOK REVIEW CONTEST

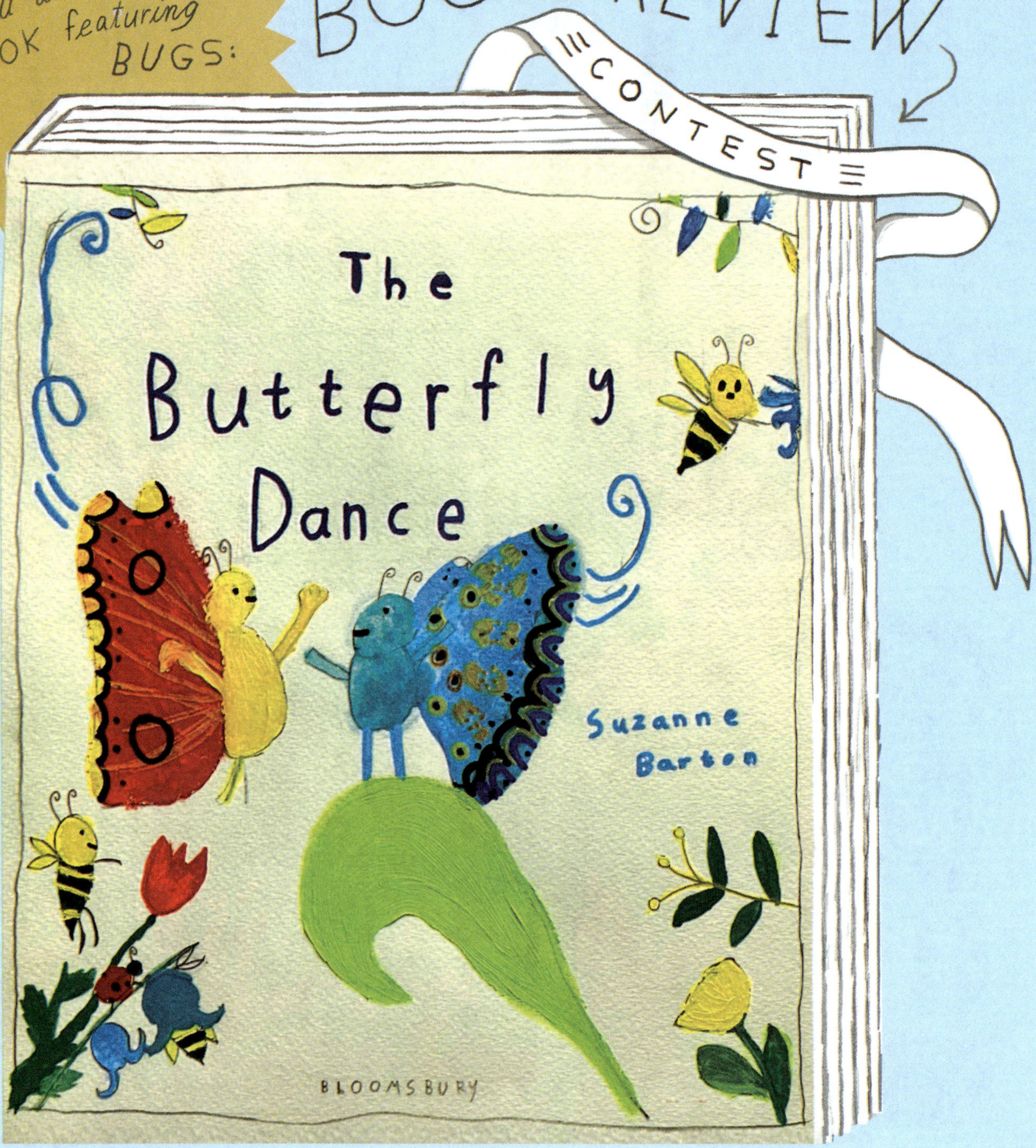
The Butterfly Dance
Suzanne Barton
BLOOMSBURY

REVIEW BY: SAYURI AGE: 7 FROM: CUPERTINO, CALIFORNIA

"This is a heartwarming story about friendship. It follows two adorable caterpillars, Stripe and Dotty, who share everything. One day, Stripe spins himself a silky hammock and falls asleep. Dotty tries to wake him up but has no luck. Eventually, she also spins her own hammock and goes to sleep. The story is special because Stripe and Dotty at first believe they should go their separate ways, thinking only the same kinds of butterflies can stay together. But they miss each other so much that they realize it doesn't matter if they are different, they can still be friends." —Sayuri

REVIEW BY: VERA AGE: 10

FROM: SAN FRANCISCO, CALIFORNIA

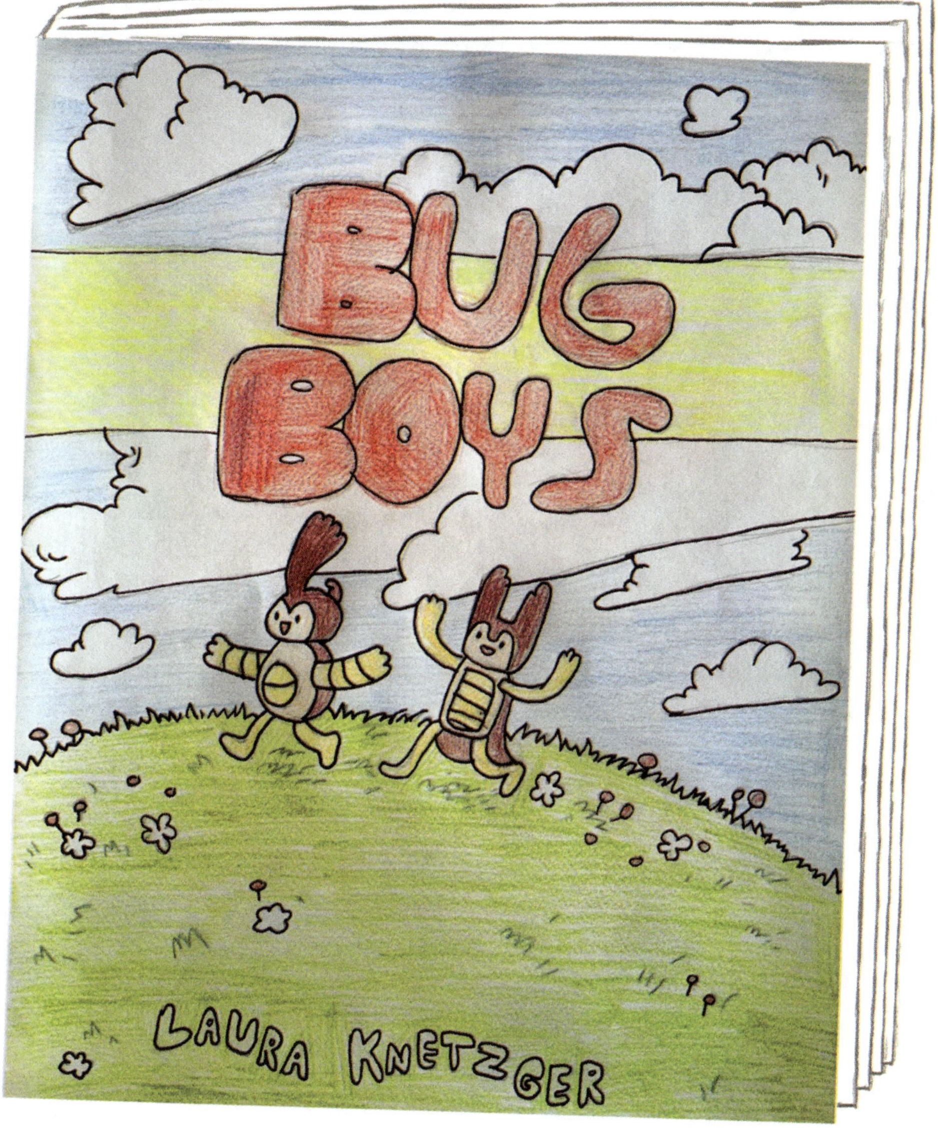
BUG BOYS
LAURA KNETZGER

"*Bug Boys* is a good book in my opinion because it has a very cozy vibe to it. The illustrations match the coziness too. It's about two boys who are bugs and are also best friends. Throughout the book they go on fun adventures and meet new people, they also fight sometimes too. In conclusion, this book is very good and fun to read." —Vera

ON OUR BOOKSHELF

Are you a fan of bugs? Join the club.
--by ELISE GRAVEL

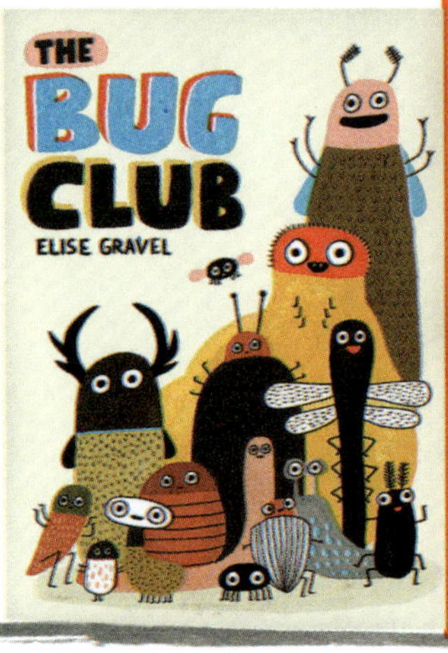
THE BUG CLUB
ELISE GRAVEL

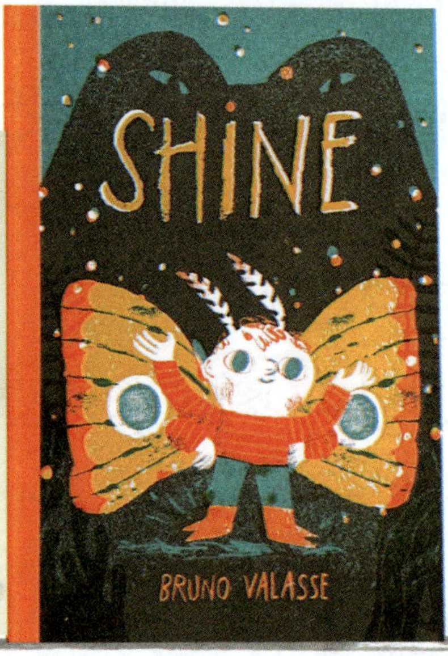
SHINE
BRUNO VALASSE

Learn from this bright little moth.

--by BRUNO VALASSE

Follow one caterpillar across three phases of life.

--by BEN CLANTON

--art by BEN CLANTON COREY R. TABOR ANDY CHOU MUSSER

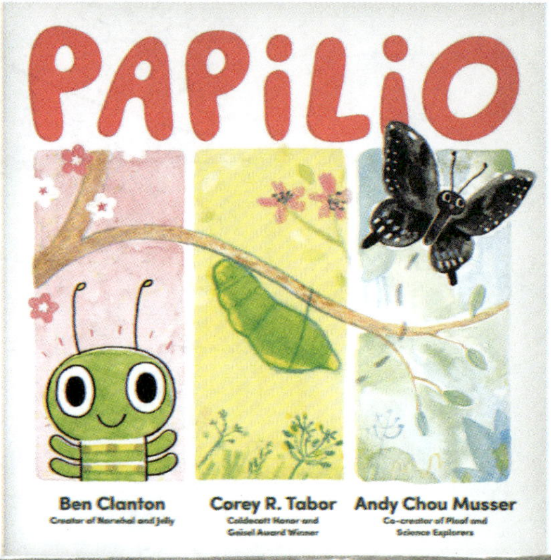
PAPILIO
Ben Clanton
Corey R. Tabor
Andy Chou Musser

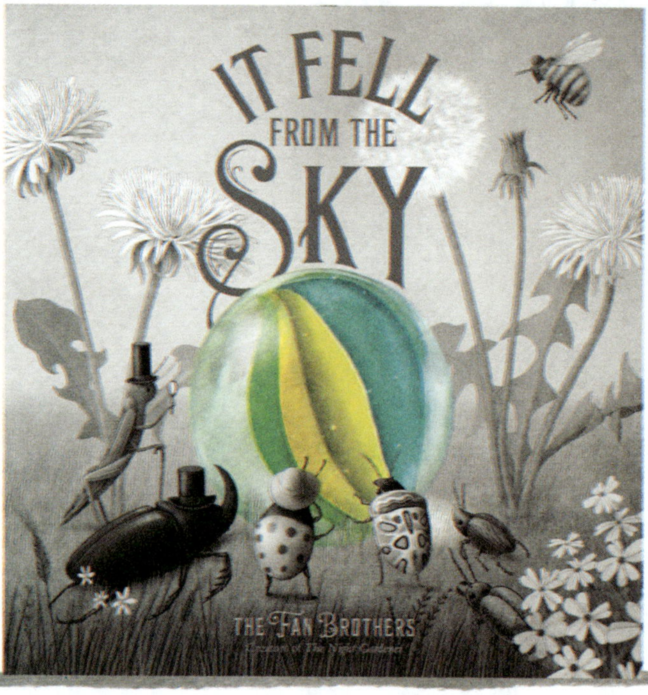
IT FELL FROM THE SKY
THE FAN BROTHERS

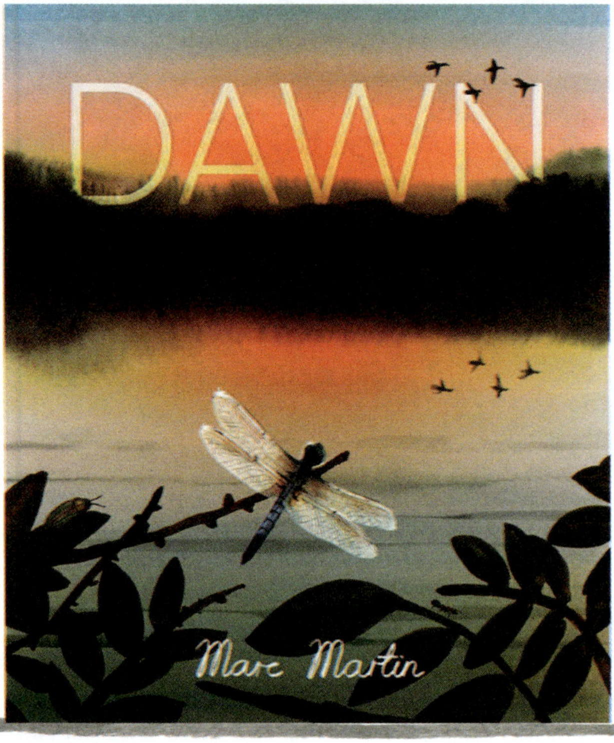
DAWN
Marc Martin

Follow a gaggle of sleuthing bugs on this micro-sized mystery.
--by THE FAN BROTHERS

An intricate portrayal of early-morning insect behavior.
--by MARC MARTIN

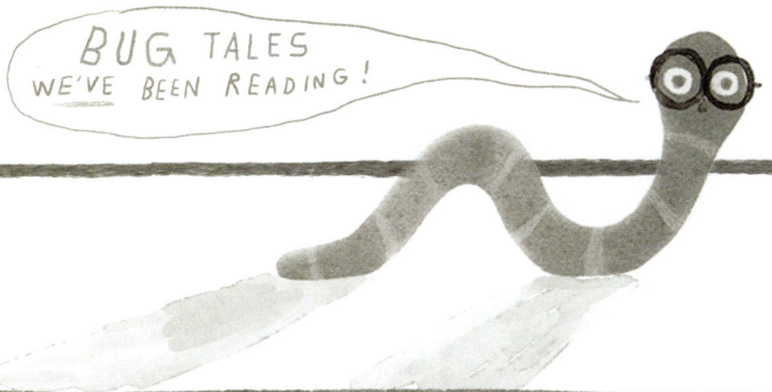
BUG TALES
WE'VE BEEN READING!

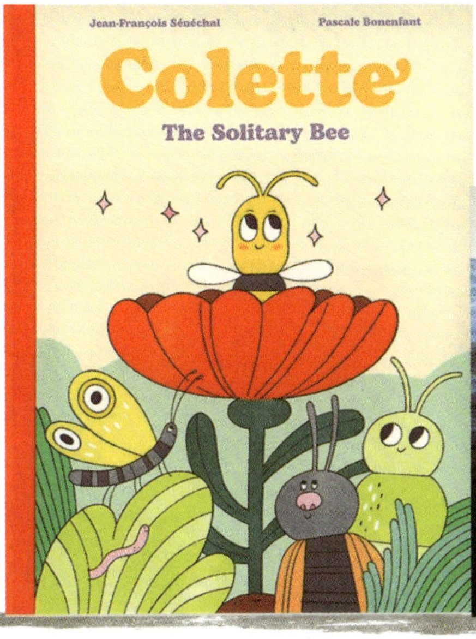
Jean-François Sénéchal
Pascale Bonenfant
Colette
The Solitary Bee

--by
JEAN-FRANÇOIS SÉNÉCHAL
--art by
PASCALE BONENFANT

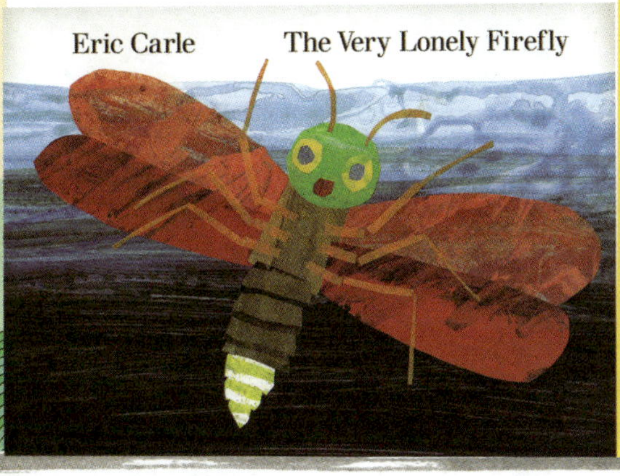
Eric Carle
The Very Lonely Firefly

--by
JULES HOWARD
--art by
GOSIA HERBA

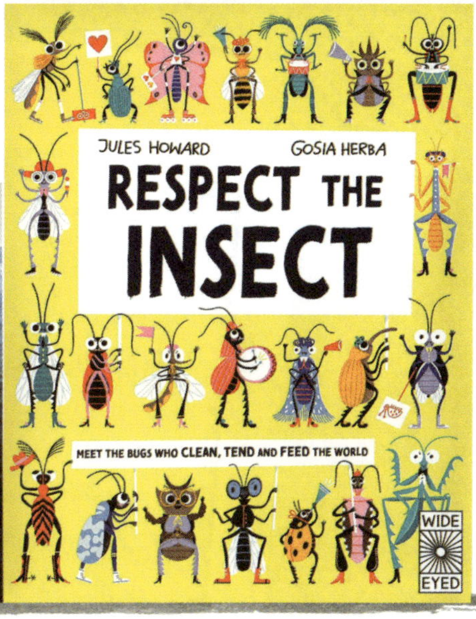
JULES HOWARD
GOSIA HERBA
RESPECT THE INSECT
MEET THE BUGS WHO CLEAN, TEND AND FEED THE WORLD
WIDE EYED

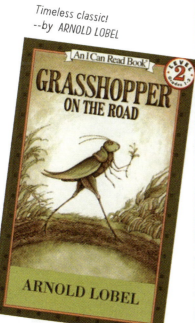

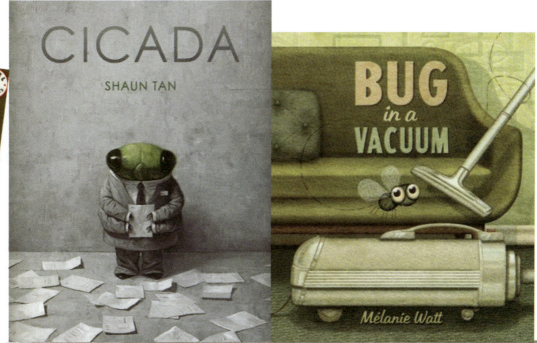

Timeless classic!
--by ARNOLD LOBEL

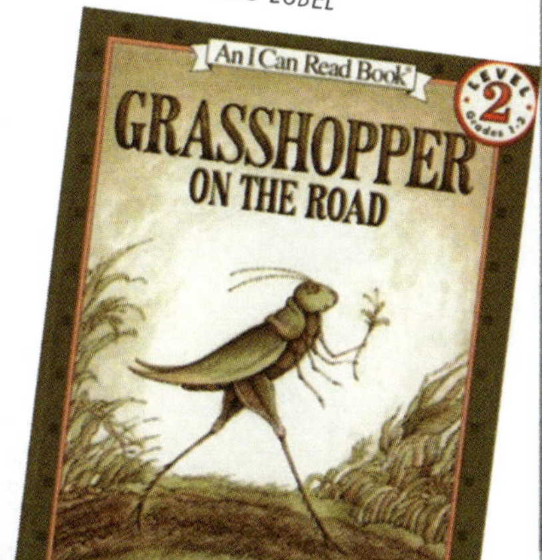
An I Can Read Book
LEVEL 2
GRASSHOPPER ON THE ROAD
ARNOLD LOBEL

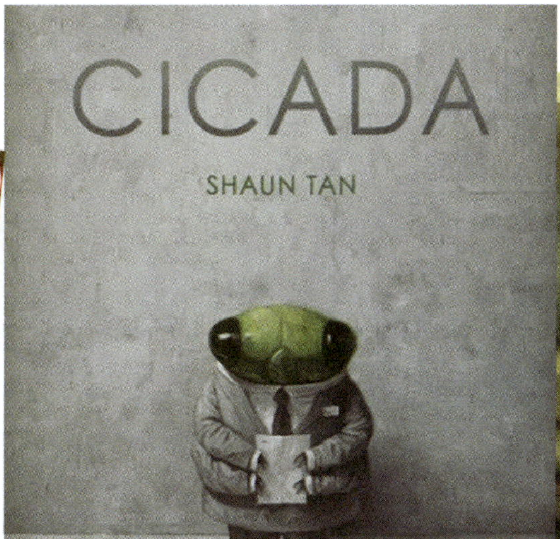
CICADA
SHAUN TAN

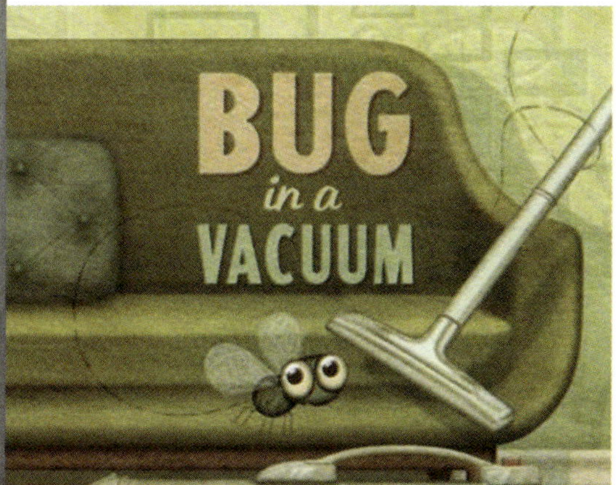
BUG in a VACUUM
Mélanie Watt

You will never look at cicadas the same way again.
--by SHAUN TAN

A delightful story found in an unexpected place.
--by MÉLANIE WATT

Deeper Dive!

Did you know about this shade of deep red paint that is made of BUGS?

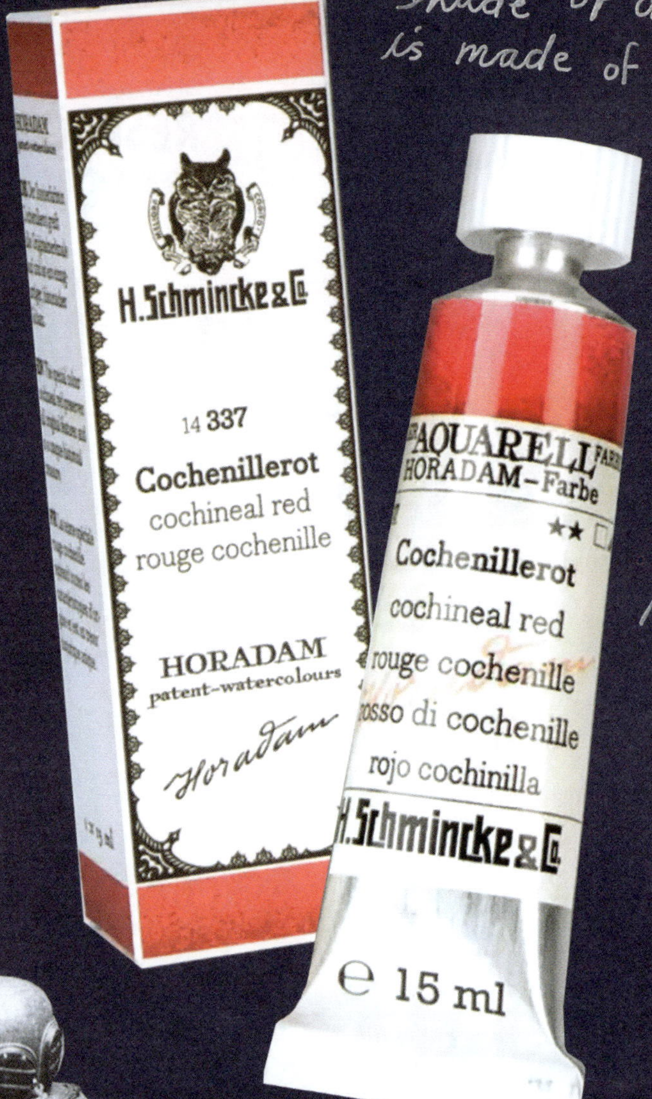
H.Schmincke&Co.
14 337
Cochenillerot
cochineal red
rouge cochenille
HORADAM
patent-watercolours
Horadam
AQUARELL
HORADAM-Farbe
Cochenillerot
cochineal red
rouge cochenille
osso di cochenille
rojo cochinilla
H.Schmincke&Co.
15 ml

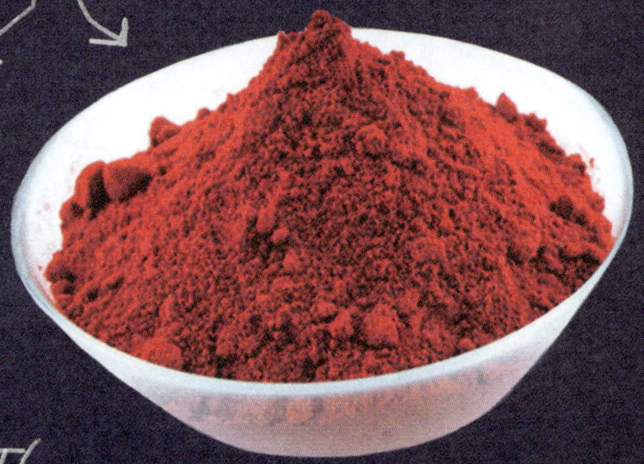

The COCHINEAL insect is harvested from the prickly pear cactus, which it lives on, parasitically.

HERE IS THE BUG UP CLOSE

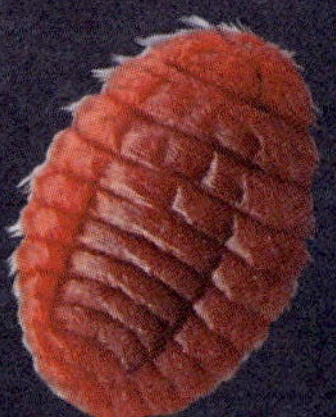

HERE IS ITS ACTUAL SIZE:

1 millimeter

PRICKLY PEAR CACTUS

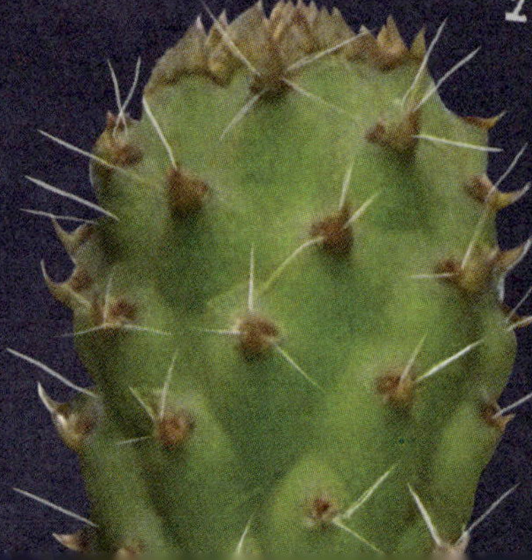

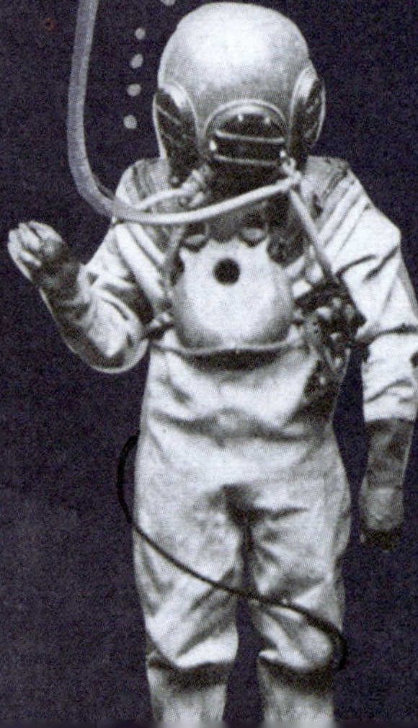

Future ENTOMOLOGISTS (← someone whose job is to study bugs) will need a handy magnifying lens to examine insects in the wild.

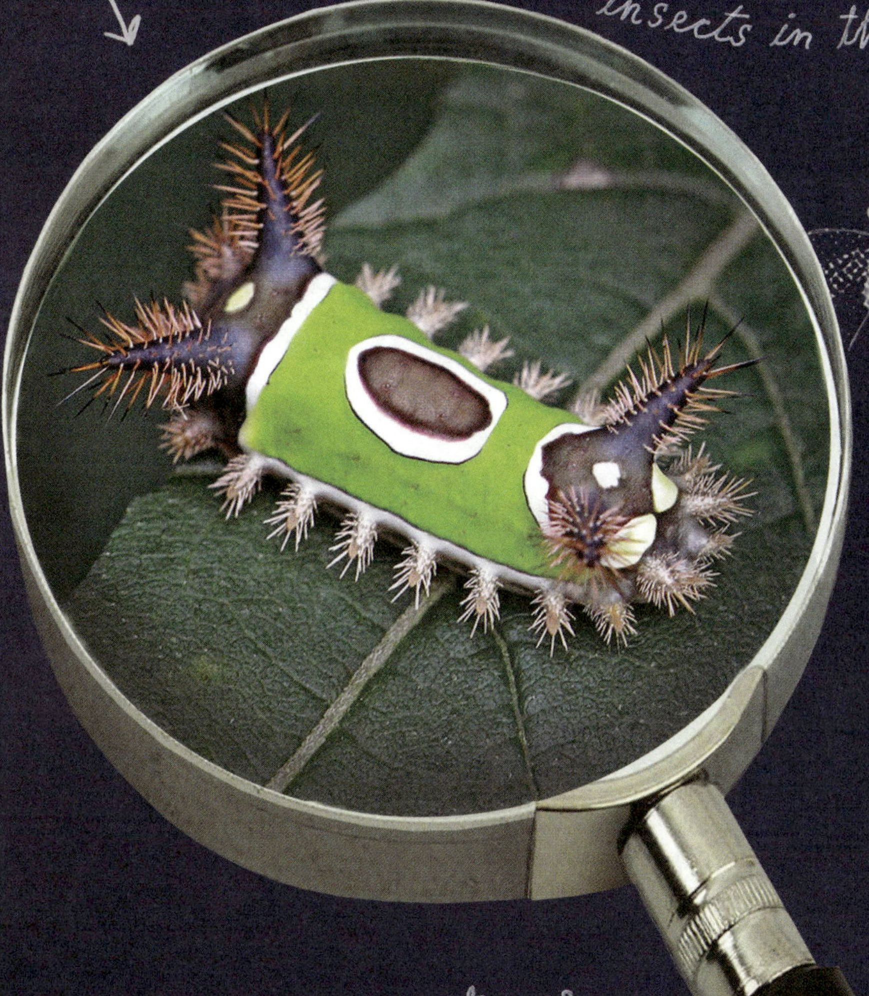

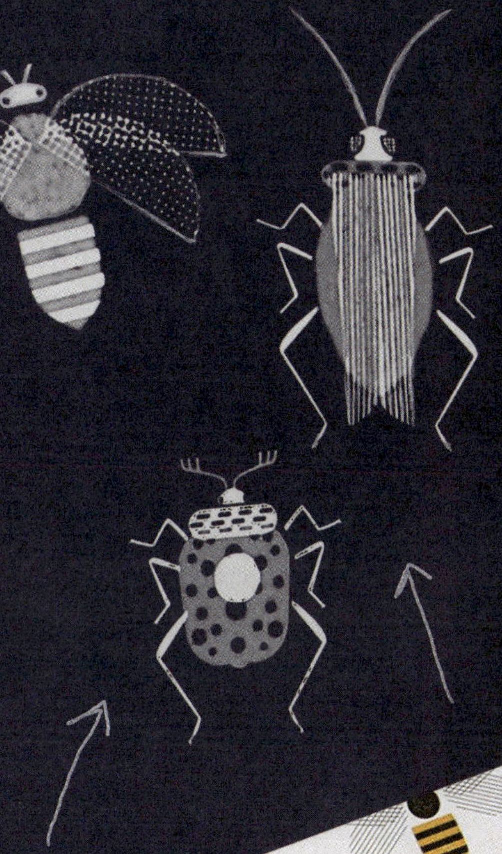

With this set of stamps, mix-and-match BUG PARTS to design your own:

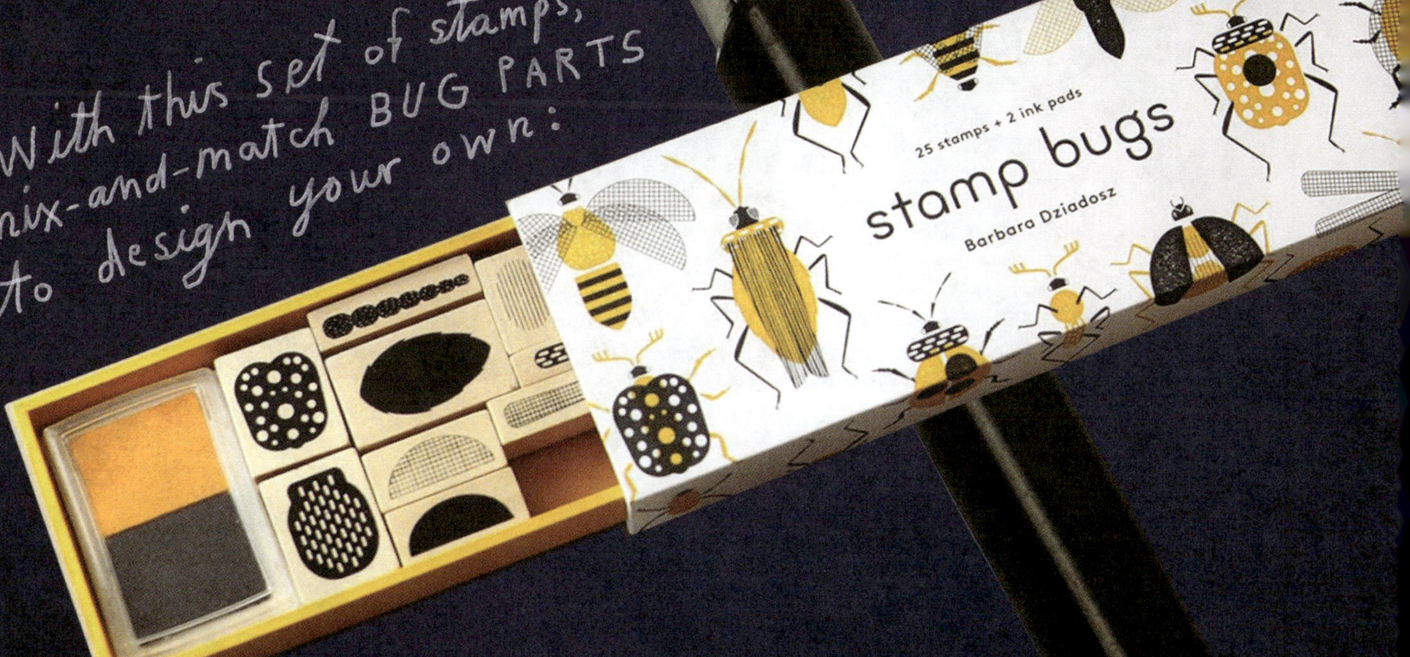
25 stamps + 2 ink pads
stamp bugs
Barbara Dziadosz

THE YOUTH WRITING IN THIS ISSUE IS BY STUDENTS FROM

Noordje, Amsterdam, Netherlands
826 MSP, Minneapolis, Minnesota

TAKE A TRIP AND VISIT!

FIND A WRITING CENTER NEAR YOU: ▶ **YOUTHWRITING.ORG**

In every issue of *Illustoria*, students from the International Alliance of Youth Writing Centers contribute their own writing and art to add a range of voices to these pages. The International Alliance is joined in a common belief that young people need places where they can write and be heard, where they can have their voices polished, published, and amplified. There are nearly seventy centers worldwide. Learn more at www.youthwriting.org.